D0015739

THE MAGICAL REALITY OF
NADIA

THE MAGICAL REALITY OF
NADIA

By **BASSEM YOUSSEF** and
CATHERINE R. DALY

Illustrated by **DOUGLAS HOLGATE**

Scholastic Inc.

WITHDRAWN

Copyright © 2021 by Little Tut, Inc.

All rights reserved. Published by Scholastic Inc., *Publishers since 1920.* SCHOLASTIC and associated logos are trademarks and/or registered trademarks of Scholastic Inc.

The publisher does not have any control over and does not assume any responsibility for author or third-party websites or their content.

No part of this publication may be reproduced, stored in a retrieval system, or transmitted in any form or by any means, electronic, mechanical, photocopying, recording, or otherwise, without written permission of the publisher. For information regarding permission, write to Scholastic Inc., Attention: Permissions Department, 557 Broadway, New York, NY 10012.

This book is a work of fiction. Names, characters, places, and incidents are either the product of the authors' imaginations or are used fictitiously, and any resemblance to actual persons, living or dead, business establishments, events, or locales is entirely coincidental.

Library of Congress Cataloging-in-Publication Data available

ISBN 978-1-338-57228-5

10 9 8 7 6 5 4 3 2 1   21 22 23 24 25

Printed in Italy   183

First edition, February 2021

Book design by Katie Fitch

Special thanks to Ava Forte Vitali and Summer Elbardissy

Dear Nadia,
Fun Fact: Your magical soul made my
reality a lot more bearable.
Love,
Baba

For Jon and Oonagh, with love.
-C.D.

For Allyson and Angus. Always.
-D.H.

Prologue

"Hello! Hello out there!" The teacher was scared. He was somewhere dark and very, very cramped. What was happening?

A minute ago, he had been standing in the shadow of the Great Pyramid, the strong Egyptian sun glinting off its golden top. In the distance he could see papyrus boats floating down the Nile River and the twin statues of Osiris towering over the temple gate. He was making a joke about his old buddy-turned-bully, the royal magician. Everyone had been laughing (as they should have been. It was a very funny joke).

But the magician had not taken it well.

"I have had enough of your insolence!" the magician had said, tearing an amulet from around his neck and thrusting it out toward the teacher. "I shall condemn you to the dark for all eternity!"

"Dramatic much?" the teacher had teased. He was bent over, he was laughing so hard. The crowd joined in.

An elderly bystander grabbed the magician's arm. "No!" he shouted. "There must be an escape. The pharaoh will insist!"

"I don't care!" bellowed the magician. "I want this fool gone forever!"

The crowd gasped at the magician's insolence. And the next thing the teacher knew, there was a great wind and a loud sucking noise. Then everything turned black.

"Help! Help!" he had screamed. But it seemed no one could hear him.

He could hear them, though. The teacher stopped yelling and strained to listen.

"Royal magician, I am sorry to do this," said a voice. "But you leave me no choice—"

The teacher couldn't hear the next part over the crowd. He pressed his ear up against the wall of . . . wherever it was he was. The voice was still speaking. The teacher caught bits of it.

". . . a way to break the spell . . . says the word . . ."

But the crowd was too noisy and the teacher couldn't hear much else. At least not until the terrified scream. That was loud and clear. Some poor other soul seemed to be suffering a fate similar to his.

Unless that was his own screaming. Was he screaming again? He checked. Nope. Not him.

Then, silence.

The teacher put his head in his hands. *What could be worse than being imprisoned for all eternity?*

Well, maybe being imprisoned for all eternity with the jingle for Scarabs R Us stuck in my head, he thought. *That song was super annoying.*

The teacher sighed.

He was going to miss his students.

And now that jingle was going to be stuck in his head. For all eternity.

Chapter One

Nadia did a slow spin in front of her bedroom mirror. The gold glitter on her brand-new Eye of Horus T-shirt sparkled in the afternoon sun.

"What do you think, Amelia?" she said. "Does this outfit say 'I'm a serious student' and also 'I appreciate and understand the importance of fashion'?"

She turned to her bookcase, where her bobbleheads were lined up, and found the Amelia Earhart one. She had always admired Amelia's style. Nadia bopped Amelia on the head and Amelia began nodding. Or bobbing. Same thing, really.

"It's official, then!" Nadia said, smiling. "Outfit for the first day of sixth grade—check!" Then she added a fun fact for . . . well, fun. "Did you know that the very first shopping mall was in ancient Rome?"

While spending the summer with her seriously stylish cousins during her family's annual trip to the motherland, aka Egypt, Nadia had realized that her fashion game needed a serious overhaul. Throwing on a "My Parents Went to a TED Talk and All I Got Was This Lousy T-shirt" shirt and a pair of leggings just wasn't going to cut it anymore.

So Nadia tackled fashion the way she did most everything else—with plenty of research. She scoured fashion magazines, blogs, Instagram accounts, and YouTube videos. She read up on classic Egyptian patterns and designs, too, because if she was going to do a style upgrade, she figured it might as well show off how much she loved her culture's history. Then she and her older cousin Shani went on an amazing shopping spree at the biggest mall in all of Cairo.

And in the middle of learning the difference between midi skirts and maxi skirts, mid-rise jeans and boyfriend jeans, Nadia picked up a lot of fashion facts. Not that she was partial to fashion facts—she loved all facts.

Nadia turned to the mirror once again. Her necklace had gotten tangled in the outfit-trying-on process, and she untwisted the chain. She hadn't taken the necklace off since she got it several weeks ago at a bazaar in Egypt. She had been wandering through the aisles when an antique, hippopotamus-shaped amulet caught her eye. (A fun fact had popped up in her brain then: Ancient Egyptians wore hippo amulets to ward off evil.)

Nadia had held the amulet up to take a closer look. "Bekam?" she asked the seller, fully expecting the tourist price. But her Arabic must have been pretty good, because the price was reasonable. Nadia handed over the money and fastened the chain around her neck. It felt *right* to be wearing it. Was it because it reminded her of her faraway family? Her roots in Egypt? Or maybe just because the hippo was totally adorable? She wasn't sure.

Nadia's phone beeped.

R u ready to meet up for 🍦?

Ya, she texted back. **C u in 10 mins?**

It was her best friend, Adam. It was their yearly tradition to go out for a treat at Ice Scream to celebrate the last day of freedom before school started.

Yup. Don't forget my silverneir!

Silverneer.

Silvoneer.

The present you brought me from Egypt.

Nadia laughed. Adam had many talents, but spelling was definitely not one of them. He was so far off that even autocorrect couldn't help him. But she could.

Haha, yeah, I'll bring your SOUVENIR

The Egyptian comic book Nadia had brought for him was sitting on her desk, next to a neat pile of brand-new school supplies. Adam was a comic book freak, and she knew he would go crazy for the Egyptian superheroes. (Fun fact: The first Arab comic ever was published in Egypt in 1923. It was called *The Boys*, or *Al-Awlad*.)

Nadia quickly changed back into her shorts and T-shirt, then stuck the comic book in the waistband of her shorts. She dug in her backpack for her wallet.

"See you later, bobble buds," she said, giving Amelia one last bop. Then she headed downstairs.

❖ ❖ ❖

Adam was peering into the ice cream display case when Nadia arrived at Ice Scream. She opened the door slowly so the bell wouldn't jangle, then snuck up behind her friend.

"Hurry up and decide, I haven't got all day," she said in a gruff voice.

Adam spun around with a frown on his face, then laughed when he saw who it was.

"Nadia!" he said. He gave her a big hug.

"I missed you, bestie," she said, hugging him back. But something felt weird. Nadia realized she was looking down at the top of Adam's curly red head, a view she had never seen before. She knew she had grown over the summer. Adam apparently had not. By the way he stood up taller when they pulled away, Nadia guessed that he had noticed, too.

"So, um, how was Egypt?" Adam asked. He seemed eager to move on.

"It was . . ." Nadia started to say. The trip had been great, as it always was. But this time, something had felt a little different, something she couldn't quite put her finger on. She tried again. "I mean, I . . ."

"Well, London was awesome!" Adam said, perking up again. "Actually, the flight over was terrible. Puke city except for me. They ran out of barf bags! I got extra chocolate chip cookies because no one but me could eat!"

The teenage girl behind the counter looked fairly nauseated herself. "Uh . . . can I help you?"

Nadia ordered first. "I'll take a hot fudge sundae with avocado ice cream, blueberry ripple, and, um, rocky road." (Fun fact: Rocky road ice cream got its name because it was created during the Great Depression.)

When it was his turn, Adam stared into the case, deep in thought. "I'll take a banana split with vanilla, chocolate, and strawberry," he finally said.

Nadia hid her smile. Her best friend had ordered the same exact thing for five years running.

Adam continued where he'd left off as they sat

down at a table. "So the guy sitting next to me must have gone through ten barf bags himself. Even one of the flight attendants got sick. It was intense."

"So what did you do once you got off the Upchuck Express?" Nadia asked, ready to change the subject.

"Oh, we stayed at this great old hotel in the center of London and we did all sorts of cool stuff, like the Tower of London. Went to a soccer match, too. That was Charlie's idea."

Over the summer, Adam's mom had married her boyfriend, Charlie. Nadia had missed the wedding because she was in Egypt. She hadn't spent too much time with Adam's new stepdad, but she figured anyone who would take his stepson along on his honeymoon had to be pretty cool.

"My favorite thing was Platform 9¾ at King's Cross Station," Adam continued.

"What's that?" Nadia asked.

Adam laughed. "I keep forgetting you never read the Harry Potter books."

"You know magic's not really my thing," Nadia reminded him.

"Right," Adam said. "Well, we also went to London Bridge—"

"Ooh!" Nadia said. "Did you know they used to display chopped-off heads on the original London Bridge?" She drew an imaginary line across her throat with her spoon.

"Cool," said Adam. He took a big bite of ice cream. "I actually made a little video of our trip. Do you want to see it?"

"Sure," Nadia said. Adam was really talented at tech stuff and his videos were usually awesome. They watched it on his phone while finishing their ice cream. But there was one thing missing, in Nadia's opinion.

"Did you see the queen?" Nadia asked. "She has two birthdays, you know. One's her real birthday and the other is her official—"

"Ah yes," Adam said. He reached into his backpack. "We didn't see Her Royal Highness in person, but . . ." He placed a Queen Elizabeth bobblehead, her arm raised in a stately wave, on the table.

Nadia let out a little squeal. "It's perfect! I'll put her in between . . . Albert Einstein and Yoda," she decided.

"So what did you get me?" Adam asked eagerly.

Nadia smiled and reached for the comic. But her grin faded—the comic wasn't there. "I must have dropped it!" she said. "Hopefully at home."

Adam looked heartbroken. "Can you at least tell me what it is?"

"Oh, um, I guess," Nadia said. "It's an Egyptian comic book." Adam's eyes lit up.

On the way home, they retraced Nadia's steps. No comic. When they reached her house, Nadia ran upstairs to search her room. Adam hung out in the living room, catching up with her mom.

Nadia carefully placed Queen Elizabeth on the shelf between Einstein and Yoda. Now where was that comic?

She sifted through the notebooks and folders on her desk. Nothing. She rummaged through the discarded outfits on the floor. Not there, either. She held her necklace as she stood back up—something she'd started doing whenever she was anxious—then tapped the queen's crowned head.

"Do you know where that comic book went?"

The queen's bobbing head indicated that she did.

"Well then, maybe you could help me, Your Highness?"

No answer. That was one un-fun fact about the bobbleheads. They never *really* answered back.

Ugh. Nadia flopped down on the bed and closed her eyes. She felt a tingle in her throat. Weird—Adam was going to be disappointed, but was she seriously going to cry over a lost comic book?

Wait. The tingle wasn't in her throat. It was on her throat, on her skin. Her eyes popped open and she looked down. Her necklace was *glowing*.

Chapter Two

Nadia closed her eyes and, after a moment, opened them again. Still glowing.

"Your Majesty," she said slowly, not taking her eyes off the necklace. "Are you seeing what I'm seeing?"

"Stinky crocodile spit!" said a voice.

Nadia whipped around to the bobbleheads. Had the queen really just answered her? Maybe this was a special electronic, talking bobblehead? But queens didn't usually talk about crocodile spit, did they? Nadia slowly approached the bookshelf.

The voice rang out again. "It's about time! I thought you'd never say the word. I've been trapped in that amulet FOREVER. Do you see how small that thing is?

Not comfortable for a weekend, let alone thousands of years!"

Now Nadia was sure it wasn't the queen. She looked around wildly. "Wh-what . . . Who are you? *Where* are you?"

"Over here, on the desk!"

"*On the desk?*"

"Yoo-hoo!" the voice said. "In your notebook!"

Nadia went over to the desk, her heart beating hard. And there, on the college-ruled pages of what was to be her math notebook, a little animated man was jumping up and down, waving wildly at her.

"Nadia?" Adam appeared in her doorway. "What's taking so long? Did you find the comic yet?"

Nadia whirled around, completely speechless, then looked back at the little man on the page. Adam couldn't see him from where he was standing. The little man stuck both thumbs into his ears and waggled his fingers at her.

"I . . . I couldn't find the comic," she told Adam. Then, without thinking twice, she shut the notebook and shoved it into one of the desk drawers, next to her stash of Egyptian candy bars. "Sorry."

She stole a glance at her necklace in the mirror. It wasn't glowing anymore.

"Aw man, I really wanna see that comic," Adam whined.

Nadia frowned. Her friend sounded so disappointed. She grabbed a candy bar. "Here, take this in the meantime. Mandolin bars are totally delicious."

"I'll be the judge of that," Adam said. He ripped open the wrapper and took a big bite.

"As it turns out, you're right," he admitted. "But I'm still holding out for the comic."

"I'll look for it tonight," Nadia promised, practically pushing him out the door.

She couldn't tell Adam what she thought she had just seen. If it was real, Adam would totally freak out . . . and she could only handle one person losing it at a time. And if it *wasn't* real, then she was imagining things. And she'd like to keep that to herself. For now, at least.

"Nadia, sah El nom ya habibti. Wake up, my love!" Nadia's mom was shaking her gently. "You'll be late for your first day of school."

Nadia bolted up and glanced at the clock. There was only half an hour until school started. With all the craziness last night, she must have forgotten to set her alarm!

She thanked her mom as she jumped out of bed. "Shukran ya, Mama!"

Nadia quickly got dressed. Just to be sure, she checked her necklace in the mirror. Not glowing.

After Adam had left the night before, Nadia had dug her notebook out of the drawer and looked for the little man, but the page was blank. Honestly, she'd been a little relieved. Magic—if that's what it was—didn't mix very well with facts. She decided she must have fallen asleep when she crashed on the bed and had a weird sugar-induced dream.

"Luck me wish," she said to the Yoda bobblehead. Then she grabbed her backpack.

Downstairs, Nadia took her lunch bag and a cereal bar from her mom, gave her dad a quick kiss on the cheek, and dashed out the front door to meet up with Adam on the corner.

"So who's your homeroom teacher?" he asked as Nadia took a big bite of the cereal bar. The class assignments had been sent out via email the night before.

"Ms. Arena," said Nadia, but it came out like "Mmmms Aruhruh."

"Who?" said Adam.

Nadia swallowed. "Sorry. Ms. Arena. You?"

"Same!"

"Awesome," Nadia said, and they began walking. "Do you know if Vikram, Sarah, or Chloe are in the class, too?"

"Vikram texted me he's in Ms. Wahl's class," Adam said. "Not sure about Sarah or Chloe."

Nadia and Adam had met Sarah, Vikram, and Chloe the year before and had quickly discovered they had a lot in common. They all were quick-witted, interested in the world around them, and took school—but not necessarily themselves—very seriously. They became a tight little group, eating lunch together every day, joining the same clubs, and hanging out after school. Vikram had even come up with a nickname for them—the Nerd Patrol.

As Nadia and Adam headed to school, they listed other students they hoped might be in their class. Andrew, Oona, and Abby. Maybe Olivia and Liam, though sometimes they could be annoying.

They were just approaching the drop-off area when a minivan door slid open and out popped a girl with long black hair and glasses.

"Sarah!" Nadia ran over and gave her a hug, then waved to Sarah's mom. "Hey, Mrs. Choi!"

"Nice outfit, Nadia!" Sarah said as they walked up to the front doors to the school. Sarah was a T-shirt-and-jeans kind of girl, but always appreciated other people's style, too.

"Thanks for noticing," Nadia said. "*Someone else* didn't."

"Notice what?" Adam said.

Nadia and Sarah rolled their eyes.

It turned out Sarah was in Ms. Arena's homeroom, too, so they all headed there together.

Ms. Arena was standing at the door to her classroom, a big tub of colorful hard candies under one arm.

"Good morning!" Ms. Arena said brightly.

"What's with the candy?" Adam asked. Nadia elbowed him. (Not-particularly-fun-but-still-important fact: First impressions matter.)

"I'm Nadia Youssef," she said, and held out her hand for Ms. Arena to shake. "And this is Adam Winter, and Sarah Choi."

Ms. Arena looked a little surprised at the formal introduction but shook Nadia's hand anyway. "Nice to meet you all." She held up the candy. "We're going to do an activity with these. Take as many candies as you'd like, but don't eat them yet."

Nadia fished around in the bowl, taking three pink candies. She hoped they were raspberry and not watermelon flavored.

Once inside, the three friends grabbed seats close together. Nadia hung her backpack on the chair and scanned the room. Bridget Mason Middle School started in fifth grade, so she already knew most of the kids. But there was one unfamiliar face at the back of the room, a boy talking to a group of popular kids. She caught Adam's eye and cocked her head at the boy.

"Who's that?" she mouthed.

Adam took a look and shrugged. "New kid?" he mouthed back.

Nadia stole a closer look. New Kid had shaggy sandy hair and blue eyes. He had a weird way of tossing his

head when his hair fell forward, but other than that he seemed normal. Judging by the other kids' laughter, he was pretty funny.

The bell rang a minute later. Once everyone was seated, Ms. Arena addressed the class.

"Welcome to sixth grade," she said. "I'm thrilled to be your teacher, and I know we've got an exciting year ahead of us. Principal Taylor will be doing the morning announcements in about ten minutes, which gives us the perfect amount of time to do a little activity. I know most of you already know each other, but we do have a new student. Plus, I don't know anything about any of you." She smiled. "You all took candies when you walked into the room. I'd like you to count them. However many you took is the number of fun facts you'll need to tell the class about yourself. We'll take thirty seconds now so everyone can think of what to say."

Sarah, who hated being put on the spot, turned to Nadia, a stricken look on her face. There was a fistful of candy clutched in her hand. Even Adam might have had a hard time coming up with that much to say about himself. Nadia gave Sarah a sympathetic look.

Nadia stared at the three candies on her own desk. She absolutely loved fun facts, but she was having trouble coming up with even a single one about herself. She was smart and focused. A good friend and a hard worker.

Always on time (with the exception of this morning). But were any of those things fun?

"I'll start," said Ms. Arena. "My name is Ms. Arena. I took three candies. Number one, I have a twin sister named Jennifer. Number two, we are identical. Number three, Jennifer and I spent the summer helping build a school in Tanzania."

That was seriously impressive. Nadia pitied whoever had to go next.

"How about you?" said Ms. Arena, pointing at Nadia, of course.

Nadia sat up straighter in her chair. "My name is Nadia. Number one, I spend my summers in Egypt. Number two, I collect facts and I win every trivia contest I've ever competed in. And number three . . ." Her mind was a complete blank. Adam turned around and gave her an encouraging look. "I have an amazing group of friends," she finished.

"Ah, I've always wanted to go to Egypt!" said Ms. Arena. "Thanks for sharing, Nadia." Then she pointed to Adam. "Would you like to go next?"

Adam had only chosen four pieces of candy, but he didn't let that limit him. "My name is Adam. Number one, I went to England on my summer vacation. My favorite thing was the Medieval Museum of Torture. You have no idea the terrible things people did to each other. But if you'd like to know, I took lots of videos.

I love videography and pretty much anything tech! Number two, I love gross things like horror movies and medieval torture museums and basically anything like that. Number three, once when I was six, I was visiting New York City with my parents and I got separated from them and instead of being scared I just rode the subway by myself for a couple of hours. When I finally got tired, I found a policeman and told him I was ready to go back to the hotel. And number four, I have my appendix in a jar in my bedroom. True story."

A couple kids grimaced but Nadia smiled. She had seen the appendix and it was actually pretty cool.

"Wow, thank you, Adam!" Ms. Arena said.

When it was Sarah's turn, she held up a lone candy. Nadia saw that she'd shoved the rest into her pocket.

"My name is Sarah and I like to surf with my dog." Sarah then smiled and popped the candy into her mouth, looking very relieved.

As they went around the room, Nadia learned a lot about her classmates. Andrew went to Taiwan four times a year to visit his grandfather and loved to visit the night markets and try different dumplings and ices. Eva had read one hundred books over the summer. Jack had won a ballroom dancing competition.

"And how about you?" asked Ms. Arena, pointing to the new kid. "This is your first year at Bridget Mason, right?" Everyone turned around to the back of the room and stared at him.

"That's right," the new boy said. He waved to the class. "Hey, my name is Jason. One thing about me is that I just moved to California from outside of Chicago. Number two is that I'm looking forward to learning how to surf. And number three, when I was ten, I got picked to do a free throw from half court at a Bulls game and I sunk it. I won season tickets."

"Oooooooooh," said the class. A popular boy named Aiden reached over and bumped fists with Jason. Adam turned around to stare. He looked seriously impressed, even though Nadia knew he thought sports were capital-B Boring. *Weird.*

"So yeah," Jason said. "California's not Chicago, but it seems pretty cool so far."

"Welcome, Jason," said Ms. Arena. "I hope that we'll help make you feel comfortable in your new home."

Nadia raised her hand. A fun fact had popped into her brain. She thought it would be nice to share it, to make New Kid feel welcome.

"Yes, Nadia?"

"Did you know that the Twinkie was invented in Chicago?" she asked. She smiled at Jason.

Jason stared at her for a moment. "What's your name again?" he finally said. "Google?"

The class exploded into laughter. Nadia gave a little

laugh, too. She knew Jason was making fun of her, but the joke was on him—she didn't mind being a human search engine. All her facts came in handy during class discussions, school projects, you name it. Her classmates and even teachers always looked to her for good ideas.

Nadia raised her eyebrows at Jason as if to say, "Yeah, and?"

But before Jason could answer, the loudspeaker clicked on.

"Good morning, students. Welcome back to Bridget Mason Middle School!" the voice rang out in a tinny tone. "For all you new students, and for any old students who may have forgotten me these last few months, this is Principal Taylor speaking. I hope you all had a fruitful summer and are ready to buckle down and make this the best school year yet! I know that the teachers and staff are eager to get started, and I hope that you are, too.

"Now I have some incredible news! The Museum of American History is celebrating their hundredth anniversary this year. To mark the occasion, they're creating a brand-new gallery."

Nadia perked up. She'd visited the museum so many times, she had her own subcollection of bobble-heads from the gift shop.

"Ooh," said Jason in a mock-excited voice. "A new gallery!"

Everyone laughed. Ms. Arena shushed them, but

Nadia could see a little smirk tugging on the corners of her mouth, despite herself.

Principal Taylor went on. "The theme of the gallery will be 'What Makes America, America,' and the museum wants to know what you, the next generation, have to say about it. Which leads me to the incredible news: Students are invited to present ideas for one of the exhibits."

"Great, more homework," muttered a girl seated across the aisle from Nadia.

"The winning idea will be made into an actual exhibit in the museum," said Principal Taylor. "The winning students will also get their names on the exhibit, along with the name of their school."

Nadia's heart skipped a beat. Getting her own exhibit would be *seriously* cool.

"And last but not least," said Principal Taylor, "the winners will get one thousand dollars in prize money, provided by an anonymous donor."

"Now you're talking!" shouted Jason. Cheers from all the classrooms in the school reverberated down the hallways, too.

"Oh, now I've got your attention, do I?" said Mr. Taylor. He chuckled. "This is an amazing opportunity for our students and our school, and I hope many of you participate. But if you want to exhib-it, you've got to be in it, so don't forget to fill out an entry form!"

He paused for laughter at his little rhyme, but most students were still chattering about the prize money. "Your teachers will share the rest of the details with you. Let's make Bridget Mason Middle School proud!" The loudspeaker clicked off.

The chattering in the room picked up. Nadia tried to catch Adam's eye to see if he wanted to work together, but he was intently staring toward the back of the room. To where Jason was sitting, Nadia realized.

"All right," Ms. Arena said. She clapped her hands to call them back to order. "I'm glad you're all so excited. Let's go over the details."

Ms. Arena rattled off the guidelines, but Nadia could barely concentrate—there were already a million ideas swirling in her brain. (Fact: She was going to win this thing.)

Chapter Three

Nadia walked into the cafeteria swinging her lunch bag, excited to chat about the contest. She scanned the room for her friends, almost immediately spotting Vikram in a hard-to-miss red shirt with white polka dots. Nadia waved and headed over.

"Hey! Nice Eye of Horus shirt, Nadia!" Vikram cried, giving her a big hug. "I bet I can guess where you got that!"

Chloe arrived next, and she and Nadia embraced.

"I love your scrunchie!" Nadia said as they pulled away.

"Thanks," Chloe said, touching the neon green hair tie holding her braids in a bun. "My mom picked it out. She's always saying my dark skin and hair make bright colors appear brighter and that I shine brighter when I wear them. Cheesy, right?"

Nadia laughed. "A little cheesy . . . but true. It's very Chloe."

Adam and Sarah showed up and their group was complete. Nadia glanced around the table and smiled. The Nerd Patrol was together again, to face another school year.

"So is this contest amazing or what?" said Nadia as she pulled out her lunch. She took a deep appreciative sniff. Her mom had packed last night's leftover koushary, a combination of rice and lentils in a tangy tomato sauce topped with chickpeas and fried onions. *Deeeelicious.* "The Nerd Patrol will be a team, right?" she asked her friends.

"I'm in," said Chloe.

"Me too," said Vikram.

"Me three," added Sarah.

"Me four," said Adam. He looked around at everyone sheepishly. "Man, we really are nerds, aren't we?"

"How did they say the winner gets chosen?" asked Vikram. "I stopped listening as soon as the prize was announced."

"Everyone has to present their exhibit idea in a creative way in the museum auditorium in two and a half weeks," Chloe informed him. "The winner will be chosen by the board of directors."

"Cool," Vikram said, unwrapping his lunch.

"Now we just need to figure out an idea for an exhibit," said Sarah. "We should meet right away—two and a half weeks is hardly any time! Too bad the special room doesn't open until next weekend."

Ms. Arena had told them how the museum was dedicating a behind-the-scenes workroom filled with all sorts of materials where kids could construct their projects.

Sarah turned to Nadia with a sly smile. "Hey, any chance we could meet at your house?"

Nadia's house was everyone's favorite place because she had a pool with a slide in her backyard. She swallowed a mouthful of koushary. "Sure, I'll ask my parents tonight. This Saturday good for everyone?"

The Nerd Patrol nodded.

All of a sudden, Adam jumped up. "Jason! Jason!" he called. "Over here!" The new boy had walked into the cafeteria. Adam began clearing a space, nearly knocking over Nadia's lunch bag in the process.

Jason spotted Adam and headed to their table.

"Thanks, Adam," he said. He sat down next to Nadia and dropped his brown paper lunch bag on the table. "Hey, it's Google Girl," he said.

Nadia smiled but decided to nip this in the bud. "Actually, could you call me Nadia?"

Jason nodded as he pulled out a foil-wrapped sandwich.

"Hey, I have a great idea," Adam said to Jason after Vikram, Sarah, and Chloe introduced themselves. "We were just talking about the contest. Why don't you join our group?"

"Oh man, I just told Aiden and Mike that I would do it with them," said Jason. "Too bad."

Adam's face fell. "Yeah, too bad."

Jason pointed to Nadia's food. "What's that?"

"It's my lunch," she said. *Duh.*

"It smells weird," Jason said. He took a closer look at Nadia. "Where exactly are you from, anyway?"

Nadia's jaw tightened. She didn't like his tone, but it wasn't the first time someone had asked her where she was from.

"I'm Egyptian," she said brightly. "And American, too; we moved here when I was six. And this"—she held up her lunch—"is koushary. It's one of my favorites. Would you like to try it?"

Jason raised his hand defensively as if she had just threatened to hit him with her lunch instead of offering him a bite. "No thanks," he said.

Nadia knew when she was being blown off. But then her mind presented her with a fun fact. "Did you know," she said slowly, "that koushary was originally an Indian dish before it was adopted by the Egyptians?"

"Koushary in the house!" said Vikram. He bumped fists with Nadia.

Jason frowned. "Well, I eat American food"—he held up his roast beef sandwich—"not desert people food."

Adam let out a little yelp of a laugh, but Vikram and Nadia exchanged a look. *Desert people food? What was that supposed to mean?* Nadia felt her cheeks turn as red as the tomatoes in her koushary, which suddenly didn't seem so appealing. What was this new kid's problem?

As the others chatted, Nadia tried to shake the icky

feeling Jason's comment left in her stomach. It didn't seem like he was trying to be mean. Maybe he was just really nervous, this being his first day in a new school?

As the others told Jason all the ins and outs of Bridget Mason, Nadia ate her koushary in silence. She even held back the fun fact that Principal Taylor had himself attended the school and if you pulled out the 1985 yearbook you could find him, in all his mulleted glory, voted Most Likely to Come Back to Teach at This School.

By the time they finished eating, Nadia felt mostly better. She scooped up the last of the spicy *koushary* sauce and licked her spoon clean. Jason balled up the foil his sandwich had been wrapped in.

"Hey, what's the difference between roast beef and pea soup?" he suddenly asked.

The friends all looked at one another. "I don't know," Sarah finally said. "What *is* the difference between roast beef and pea soup?"

Jason grinned. "Anyone can roast beef!"

The table was quiet as everyone let the punch line sink in. Then there was a strangled sound as Adam started choking on his chocolate milk, he was laughing so hard. Nadia couldn't help it—she let out a giggle, too, and pretty soon everyone else joined in.

"Oh wow," Adam said once he could talk again. "That almost came out my nose!"

"So," said Nadia's father that night at dinner, "what was the most exciting thing that happened today?"

Nadia smiled. Baba never asked boring questions like "How was your day?" Sometimes he asked her to tell him the funniest thing. Or the most surprising. And he and Mama usually had pretty good stories to share themselves—they were both surgeons at the same hospital. Baba was a cardiologist and Mama was a pulmonologist. They liked to joke that between them they had everything within the rib cage covered.

"They announced this amazing contest!" Nadia said. She filled them in on all the details, barely pausing to take a breath. "So can the Nerd Patrol come over on Saturday so we can figure out our idea for the contest?"

"Of course," her mom said. "You know we love your friends."

"Awesome!" Nadia said. She took a huge bite of her fried chicken leg and chewed as fast as she could. Mama's cooking, whether Egyptian or American, was delicious, but Nadia didn't have time to savor her meal—she had work to do. She'd been trying to think of a perfect idea for the contest all day, but so far, she hadn't come up with much. The theme was so broad—there must have been a million things they could focus on.

"Can I be excused?" she asked five minutes later. "I want to keep brainstorming."

"Have you finished all your homework?" Baba asked.

Ugh. No. That was her parents' rule—no other activities until she'd finished her homework.

"And you haven't cleared the table yet," Mama added.

Nadia sighed. "Fair enough."

"Tell you what, habibti," Baba said, "we'll clear the dishes while you finish your schoolwork, okay?" He winked.

(Fact: Baba was the best.)

Nadia brought her backpack over to the table while her parents started clearing the dishes, then pulled out her math notebook and got to work. The first few problems went quickly, but she got stuck on the last one. Her pencil tip broke as if it was just as frustrated as she was.

She leaned down to grab another pencil from her backpack, moving her necklace out of the way as it swung forward, and called out to her father. "Hey, Baba, could you help me with this last math problem?"

$$\frac{1}{2} + \frac{2}{3} =$$

$$\frac{1}{3} + \frac{1}{4} =$$

"Sure," Baba called, "just as soon as I finish loading the dishwasher."

Nadia sat back up and pulled her notebook closer . . . and saw that little man again!

"Yo!" he said, nodding

his chin at her. "What's up?"

"Aaaaaaahhhhh!" Nadia screamed, and slammed the notebook shut, knocking over her water glass.

Baba came rushing in, a dish towel thrown over his shoulder and a look of pure panic on his face. "What's wrong?"

"Um . . . nothing," said Nadia, clutching the notebook to her chest. "I knocked over my water, that's all." Her dad used the dish towel to mop it up.

"No use screaming over spilled water," he said.

Nadia gave him a weak grin. Her dad knew the American idiom was "no use crying over spilled milk," but he liked to purposely bungle up idioms to make her laugh. It helped him practice his English, too.

"Do you still need help with your math problem?" he asked once the table was dry.

"No," said Nadia so forcefully her father flinched. "I mean, I figured it out already. I mean, I think I'll go upstairs." She grabbed her notebook and pencil. "Good night, Baba."

Her mind raced as she rocketed up the stairs. This was not a dream. This was really happening. There was a little animated man haunting her math notebook!

Unless she was losing it. That was still definitely a possibility.

Chapter Four

Nadia threw the math notebook onto her desk. She was going to get to the bottom of this. She flipped open the cover and . . .

. . . it was just her math homework.

"Ugh! Stupid math!" she said. She grabbed the notebook and flung it against the bookcase. The bobbleheads started bobbing madly. Einstein seemed to be doing it in an almost judgmental way.

"Sorry," Nadia said to him, softening. "Math's not stupid, but . . . maybe I am? I mean, come on—a little animated man! It's ridiculous, right?!"

Logic. Details. Facts. These were Nadia's specialties. There was no way to reasonably explain an animated man talking to her from the pages of a notebook.

"But I know I saw him," Nadia said stubbornly. "And heard him."

By habit, her hand went to her throat and the amulet.

"Wait!" she said. "The amulet . . . the first time the little man appeared, he said he was inside it!" Maybe she had somehow summoned him with her necklace?

She tightened her grip on the hippo.

Still no little man.

The bobbleheads were mostly still now, but Jane Austen was slowly bobbing.

"Do you have any words of wisdom, Jane?" Nadia asked. "Because I'm— Wait! He also said something about a word, didn't he? There must be a magic word!"

Her hand still on the necklace, Nadia recalled some words that had been spoken aloud when he appeared before. "Baba!" she said. "Math!"

Nothing.

"Homework?"

Still nothing.

She tried again. "Dishwasher?"

Nadia let out a giant sigh. Maybe she really was imagining things. "I need some help," she muttered.

At once, Nadia's necklace tingled and glowed. And before her amazed eyes, the little man she had seen before appeared in her notebook again.

"Blustering beetles!" the little man said, shaking his fist at Nadia. "Are you going to slam this thing shut again? Give me a little warning this time, will ya? I'll take cover under one of these math problems or something." He pointed to the problem Nadia had tried to solve and erased several times. "Huh! Look at that! Thousands of years later and fractions are still giving students conniptions!" He laughed.

Nadia's legs were shaking. She sat down in her desk chair and put the notebook in front of her. The little man was now doing knee bends and lunges while gazing around at Nadia's room.

"So this is America?" he asked. "Frankly, I'm a little disappointed. Where are the purple mountain majesties? The amber waves of grain?" He suddenly stood up tall and broke into song. "Oh, beauuuuuuuuutiful for spaaaaaacious . . ."

Nadia swallowed. Should she talk back to him? It wasn't any weirder than talking to her bobbleheads, right? Maybe it would stop him from singing—he sounded like her neighbor's elderly cat.

"Um, well," Nadia said, cutting him off. "This is my bedroom, which technically is in America, yes. But . . . um . . . who are you?"

"Ah . . . now we're getting somewhere," said the man. He did a fancy little bow. "The name is Titi. I am an ancient Egyptian teacher who ticked off the wrong royal magician, hence being confined to that amulet for all eternity." He pointed to her necklace, then dramatically grabbed his heart. "Great Giza is THAT what I've been living in all these centuries? A stinky *hippopotamus*?"

Nadia glanced down at her necklace. "I mean, I guess?" she said. "But I thought hippos were considered sacred in ancient Egypt—"

"Yeah, yeah," Titi said. "But, boy, do they stink!" He sniffed his armpits self-consciously, then looked desperately to Nadia. "Do I smell? I don't smell, Nadia, do I? Oh, where is some frankincense when you need it?"

Nadia leaned in to sniff the page but then paused, her eyes wide. "How do you know my name?!"

Titi shrugged. "I've been hanging around your neck for a few weeks now. I know a lot about you."

Nadia's mouth fell open. That sounded kind of creepy.

"Oh, close your mouth," he said. "You look like Hatmehit's hat! Hatmehit was an ancient Egyptian fish goddess," he explained.

Nadia snapped her mouth shut. "I know that." (Fun fact: Hatmehit's "hat" was a catfish.) "So you know a lot about me. But back to you. You were in the hippo . . . but now you're not in the hippo. You're here. In my math notebook."

"Righto," Titi said. "I was in the hippo." He looked

at the amulet again. "Actually, I've got the sneaking suspicion that I was in the *back half* of the hippo. That blasted royal magician couldn't even banish me to a *whole* hippo . . ." His voice trailed off, a faraway look on his face.

Nadia snapped her fingers. "Um . . . yeah. We've established you were in the hippo. How did you get out of the hippo?"

"Oh!" Titi said. "Yes. Apparently, I needed someone to get their hands on the amulet and say the magic word—"

"So there *is* a magic word!" Nadia said. "What is it?!"

Titi shrugged. "Don't you know? You're the one who said it."

Nadia shook her head.

"Huh," Titi said. "We'll have to work on that. But I guess I just needed the right person to hold the necklace and say the word, and apparently that person is you." He looked her up and down. "I guess you'll do."

"Well!" Nadia said, frowning. "If that's how you're going to treat me . . ." She reached forward to close the notebook.

"No, no, no, just kidding!" Titi said. "I'm so happy to be free! You have no idea how awful it was being stuck in that necklace. I've been there for thousands of years. It was terrible! Did I happen to mention I've been

in there for thousands of years? Quite possibly confined to the butt area?"

"You certainly did," said Nadia. She took the notebook and sat down on the floor, grabbing a pillow to get comfy. She was starting to feel she might be there awhile.

"I'll give you a tiny idea of how horrible it was in there," Titi said. "Have you ever been in the car with your parents and you get caught in terrible traffic with no end in sight and your phone dies and you don't have a charger and your parents are listening to the oldies station passionately singing along to 'Total Eclipse of the Heart' and people in other cars are staring at you and you want to disappear and think to yourself, *Well, at least things can't get any worse*, and then you suddenly realize that you really have to pee?"

Nadia scowled at him. "Have you been spying on me?"

"That's beside the point!" he said. "You thought that situation was the worst thing ever, but my situation was a million, billion, trillion times worse than that."

"Okay, I get it," said Nadia. "But it couldn't have all been bad. I bet you've seen some pretty cool things over the years."

"Heard," Titi said, pointing to his ear. "I couldn't see anything while trapped in that . . . corpulent creature. But I could hear everything that was going on around whoever was wearing it."

"Gotcha," Nadia said. "So who had the amulet before me? And before that? Ooh! Have you ever hung around the neck of someone famous?"

"Oh yes," Titi said. "Have you heard of Justin Bieber?"

"You hung around Justin Bieber's neck?!" Nadia squealed.

"No," Titi said, "thank goodness. Can't stand him. Kids don't still listen to him, do they?"

"Not really," Nadia said. "He got old and weird."

"I beliebe it," Titi said. "Anyway, I hung around the neck of the fourth-century equivalent of the Biebs. Let me tell you, he was hip, he played the lute like nobody's business, and he wore a funky turban that drove the girls crazy. But the sultan—he totally hated the kid's voice. So he did the ancient version of the YouTube dislike button." Titi dragged his finger across his throat.

"Harsh," said Nadia.

"Tell me about it," said Titi. "And after that, I got lost in the sewers of Cairo for a couple hundred years. Which is maybe why I'm partial to grunge music now?"

Nadia groaned. Apparently even ancient Egyptian teachers told dad jokes.

"Okay," Nadia said. "So you were stuck in the amulet for a long time. But now you're free."

"Free enough," Titi said. "But I seem to be only two-dimensional." He spread his arms out. "And it looks like I can only appear on paper. Lame."

"I wonder why that is," said Nadia.

Titi thought for a minute. "Maybe because I was a teacher? I was in charge of training the new scribes to read, write, and do math. We used a lot of papyrus, which was the ancient Egyptian version of—"

"Paper, I know," said Nadia. "That makes sense, then." She burst into laughter. None of this made any sense at all!

"So, what's next?" she asked. "Do you ever get to become a real boy?"

"Ha ha ha," said Titi sarcastically.

"You know what I mean," said Nadia. "You're a cartoon. Will you ever be a human again?" She thought for a moment. "Ooh! Do you have powers? What kind?"

Titi crossed his arms, closed his eyes, and thought hard. "Yeah, I don't know," he finally said. "But I am getting this feeling like something has to happen seven times for me to be free. Seven was a very important number in ancient Egypt, you know."

"I know," Nadia said. (Fun fact: The number seven symbolized completion in ancient Egyptian mythology.) "Maybe it's wishes—you know, like in *Aladdin*."

Titi grew very serious. "Are you comparing me to a fictional character from a fairy tale? How insulting!"

Nadia looked down at the animated character in her notebook. "I mean, you have to admit there are some similarities."

Titi jumped over to the margin. "Okay, okay, I see your point. But still, clearly seven wishes are way better than the three that Aladdin got. Should we try it? Wish for something." He waved his hands dramatically.

Nadia felt put on the spot. "Oh, um . . . I wish for . . ." Her eyes fell on her alarm clock. "My clock to turn into chocolate," she said.

"Wow," Titi said. "I can see that you are a girl who thinks BIG. But your wish is my command. Well, maybe it is. We'll see. Here goes!" He closed his eyes. He scrunched up his face. He waggled his fingers. "Um . . .

hickory dickory dock, make chocolate out of this clock!"

They both stared at the alarm clock. It ticked on, unchanged.

"I guess it's not wishes," Titi said. "Whatever! Just being out of that amulet is enough for now! Oh, sweet freedom!" He jumped up and did two handsprings . . . and then ran out of room on the page. He bounced off the spiral edge and landed with a thud next to the last math problem.

"Huh. Apparently, I can only appear on this paper," Titi said, rubbing his head where he'd bumped it. "I don't remember math being this hard."

"Well," Nadia said, "that math problem is hard. Hey! You're a teacher. Can you help me solve it?"

"Could I?!" Titi said, a big grin on his face. He jumped up and did a spin. "Oh, to have a student again! To impart wisdom on a young mind!"

Nadia rolled her eyes and let out a sigh, which turned into a yawn. No wonder she usually avoided magic; this was exhausting.

Five minutes later, the problem was solved.

"I knew you could do it!" Titi said. He jumped up and began doing handsprings again.

"Watch out!" Nadia said as he neared the spiral, but to her surprise, it didn't stop him this time. He flipped right off the edge of the page . . . and onto a worksheet sticking out of her backpack. He struck a pose reminiscent of an Olympic gymnast.

"And Titi nails the landing!" he cheered. Then he realized where he was, and his eyes went wide. "Well, build me a pyramid and call me Khufu!" he shouted.

"How did you do that?!" Nadia asked.

"I have no idea!" said Titi. "I mean, just five seconds ago I couldn't leave the notebook page. It makes no sense. Unless . . ."

"Unless what?" asked Nadia.

"Unless it's because I'm a teacher," he said slowly. He smiled. "Suffering sphinxes! Of course! It's my life's work to help students solve problems."

Nadia nodded. "And you helped me solve that math problem . . ."

". . . so now I have more freedom. Now I can appear on *any* paper. That must mean I'm closer to being free! Waaaaahooooo!"

Nadia stared as Titi began to bounce around the room. He popped up on the cover of a book on the floor.

"Was this book any good?" he asked. "No, never mind. Don't care."

He bounced to the kitten poster Nadia got from the book club in second grade that said HANG IN THERE, BABY.

"Here, kitty, kitty," Titi said. Nadia giggled. Then he bounced over to a self-portrait Nadia had done in first grade.

"Was this your abstract period?" he asked, pointing to her oversized head.

"Very funny," said Nadia. "I was six." All Titi's bouncing was making her dizzy. "Can you sit still for one minute?"

Titi came to rest on a postcard pinned to Nadia's bulletin board. "So if I help you find the solutions to seven problems—well, actually six now—I'll be free!" He hopped back to her notebook. "Do you have any more math homework?" He rubbed his hands together with glee. "I could be free by bedtime!"

"Hold up," Nadia said, grabbing the notebook and putting it on her desk. "I'm not wasting my six solutions on math."

Titi's face fell and Nadia suddenly felt bad.

"But I promise," she said, "I'll help free you. I'm sure I can find six problems I need help solving."

She was in middle school, after all. Middle school was full of problems.

Chapter Five

"I still think we should do our project on American food," Vikram said. "Hamburgers and hot dogs and apple pie, you know? Everyone loves that stuff."

"Nobody likes that idea but you," Chloe said. "Who cares that much about hot dogs?"

"Actually, hot dogs can be pretty interesting," Nadia said. "Did you know that a competitive eater named Joey Chestnut ate seventy-four hot dogs in ten minutes during the 2018 Nathan's Famous Hot Dog Eating Contest—"

"See, I told you!" said Vikram.

"—but I agree that it's not the best idea for this project," Nadia concluded.

Vikram scowled. Sarah rolled her eyes and looked longingly over at the pool.

"Maybe we should take a break?" she suggested. "Come back to this later?"

"Sounds good to me!" Adam said, already hopping up.

Nadia got up from the table. This meeting was not going as planned. They had to turn in an entry form with their idea during homeroom on Monday, and they weren't any closer than when they started brainstorming an hour ago.

Adam bounced on the end of the diving board. "Hey, Nadia!" he called. "Did you find my comic book yet? I want to show it to Jason!"

"Not yet!" said Nadia. *Ugh. Jason.* While she had to admit that Jason could be funny, he was also starting to get on her nerves. His jokes made people laugh, but they could be a little hurtful, too.

With a sigh she headed inside to look for the comic book. Again.

"Hey, guys," she said to her bobbleheads. She bopped Sherlock Holmes on the head.

But Sherlock just stared back at her blankly. Nadia sighed. The bobbleheads weren't going to be much company as she searched.

But she *did* know someone who would be! And last night, she and Titi had finally figured out what the magic word was, after plenty of trial and error. She grabbed the hippo and said, "Help!"

Titi appeared on the kitten poster. He jumped up, trying to reach the branch the kitten was hanging from. He was always eager to stretch and move after popping out of the amulet.

Nadia asked something that had suddenly come to mind. "Hey, how come the magic word is in English? English didn't even exist two thousand years ago."

"Good question," Titi said. He scrunched up his face in concentration. A moment later, a light bulb appeared over his head on the kitten poster. "Maybe . . . Well, I—a man of scholarly disposition—learned English over the years by listening to people from inside the amulet. Maybe the hippo magic spell that put me in there somehow learned it, too?"

Nadia pondered that, but thinking about magic made her brain hurt. She shook her head to clear her thoughts. Why had she come up here anyway? *Oh yeah.* "Wanna help me look for the comic book I brought back for Adam?" she asked Titi.

"Solution number two!" Titi crowed. "Hold on!" He disappeared from the kitten poster.

"No, no, no!" Nadia cried. She didn't want to waste one of her six remaining solutions on a stupid comic book! "That's not what I—"

"Too late," said Titi. His voice sounded muffled.

Nadia glanced around but didn't see him in any of his usual spots.

"Under the desk," Titi said.

Nadia reached under the desk and her hand touched the comic book. She pulled it out.

"Hey there," Titi said, waving from the cover; then he sneezed, loudly. "You should really dust under there more often, Nadia."

Nadia gave him a look. "Well, I'm glad to have the comic," she said. "But I can't believe I wasted . . ." Her voice trailed off as she tried to look on the bright side of things. "Did you get another new power?" she asked hopefully.

Titi shrugged. "Maybe. Time will tell." He popped over to her wall calendar. "So that meeting with your friends sounded really frustrating."

Nadia sighed. "Yeah. I usually have so many good ideas, but I'm feeling off my game. What Makes America, America—could that be any broader?"

"What Makes America, America," Titi mused. "I've been thinking about this. Supersized food? Deep-fried candy bars? Calling a game where you use your hands 'football' and a game where you use your feet 'soccer'? Short vacations? Free refills on sugary drin—" He stopped suddenly.

"What's up?" asked Nadia.

"I think I know what my new power is!" he said with a grin. "And I think I can help you with your project. Shall we give it a go?"

"Um . . . would it be using one of my solutions?"

Titi put his hands on his hips. "So you don't want the new exhibit at the museum to have your name on it?"

Nadia sighed. "Fine." She looked out the window. Her friends were floating around in the pool. They didn't seem to miss her.

"Awesome," Titi said. "Because this is going to be epic. Hang on!"

WHOOSH!

The room was suddenly filled with a loud blast of wind that drowned out Nadia's screams. She was falling . . . falling . . . falling. And then suddenly she was not falling anymore. The air was hot, and she seemed to be standing in . . . sand? Nadia looked around wildly. What was going on?

TITI'S TOP TEN REASONS WHY EGYPT IS THE COOLEST SUBJECT FOR YOUR PRESENTATION:

FUN FACT 1: THE BANDAGES ON AN ANCIENT EGYPTIAN MUMMY COULD BE A MILE LONG!

FUN FACT 2: BOTH MEN AND WOMEN WORE MAKEUP.

FUN FACT 3: ANCIENT EGYPTIANS INVENTED TOOTHPASTE, THE 365-DAY CALENDAR, AND WRITING.

FUN FACT 4: THE PYRAMIDS WEREN'T SAFE FROM GRAFFITI ARTISTS, EVEN IN ANCIENT TIMES.

FUN FACT 5: SOME ANCIENT TOMBS HAD TOILETS.

FUN FACT 6: ANCIENT EGYPTIANS MUMMIFIED THEIR CATS.

FUN FACT 7: KING TUT HAD A SOLID-GOLD BED.

FUN FACT 8: PYRAMID STONES COULD WEIGH UP TO 2.5 TONS EACH.

It took a minute for Nadia to catch her breath. "Whoa! That was *awesome!*" she said. "I didn't even know some of those facts!"

Titi beamed from the open comic book as he brushed sand off his feet.

"Wait," Nadia said, her mind suddenly swirling with possibilities. "Can you take me anywhere in history in that comic book? Victorian England? The Ming Dynasty?"

Titi paused. "Not sure. Should we try it? Yes, let's! Get ready for the WHOOSH-ing. One . . . two . . ."

Nadia braced herself.

"Three!" Titi shouted.

And nothing happened.

Titi shrugged. "Looks like I'm limited to ancient Egypt. But isn't that enough, Nadia? I mean, really."

"Ancient Egypt is pretty cool," replied Nadia. "All right. You've convinced me. We should do our project on ancient Egypt. But . . . one problem—how does that relate to America?"

Titi raised his eyebrows. "You're American, aren't you?"

Nadia nodded. *And* she was Egyptian.

"Clever," she said. "So it would show how Egyptian culture has influenced American culture or something like that?"

"Something like that," Titi said. "I'm sure you'll figure it out."

"Okay," said Nadia.

"So why don't you bring me down to meet your friends?" Titi asked. "Once I take them to ancient Egypt, they'll definitely be on board."

Nadia considered this. She loved her friends, but this might be too weird, even for the Nerd Patrol. What if they told other people? Plus, this whole problem-solving thing was turning out to be pretty useful. If she shared Titi, the others might use up all her solutions. She shook her head. "No way."

Titi stuck out his lower lip in a pout.

"Sorry," Nadia said. "You'll have to go back into the amulet for now. Ready?" She paused to let Titi prepare himself. They had figured out that the way to send Titi back into the amulet was to shut a book (or notebook) on him. It felt a little harsh at first, but they were both getting used to it. They even had a catchphrase.

Titi struck a pose, feet apart, one hand on a hip, the other with a fist in the air. "To the hippo and beyond!"

"To the hippo and beyond!" Nadia said, and closed the comic. She picked it up to take it down to Adam, but then thought better of it. She wasn't sure if Titi could do his magic in any book or just this one, but she wasn't about to give up the chance to travel to ancient Egypt again. That was seriously amazing.

Back outside, Baba was grilling hamburgers, hot

dogs, and kofta. Everyone was gathered around the picnic table.

"Well, I've got the perfect idea for the project," Nadia announced, grabbing a paper plate. "Egypt!"

Sarah, Vikram, and Adam just stared at her.

"Egypt?" said Chloe.

"I don't get it," Adam said.

"Me neither," added Vikram.

Nadia explained that they could do a project on how Egyptian culture—maybe even an Egyptian immigrant—had contributed to American culture. "Great, right?"

"But . . . how does that relate to the rest of us?" Sarah asked. "We're not Egyptian."

Oh. Nadia hadn't really thought that through. For a moment there, she'd sort of forgotten she was part of a group.

She thought fast. "I mean, since we all have different backgrounds—Egyptian, Korean, Indian, Jamaican—we can focus on a few different ones."

"Interesting," said Vikram.

"Hmm," Sarah said. "That could maybe work."

Chloe considered the idea, then shrugged.

Nadia turned to Adam. He had a puzzled look on his face.

"What's wrong, Adam?" asked Sarah.

Adam shrugged. "It's a cool idea, I guess. It's just

that I don't exactly know where I'm from. Maybe Switzerland? I might be a little Italian. I'm not sure."

"You just need to do some research!" Nadia said. "Ask your mom." She turned to the rest of the group. "Maybe we can each come up with . . . say, three immigrants from the country our family is from and then decide which ones we should focus on? Then we can help each other come up with a cool way of presenting it all." She smiled at her friends. "Sound good?"

Chloe shrugged again. "I guess."

Adam did not look convinced, but he didn't argue, either.

"All right, then," Nadia said with a nod.

As she reached for a piece of kofta, her necklace twinkled in the sunlight. "Thank you, Titi," she whispered.

She had an amazing group, a no-fail idea, and a little magic man to help her solve any problem that might get in the way of winning this thing. What could possibly go wrong?

Chapter Six

Thank you, Nadia," said Ms. Arena as Nadia handed her the Nerd Patrol's entry form.

Nadia had sent a group text out yesterday after realizing they hadn't decided on a leader for their group. When no one else replied within five minutes, she went ahead and filled out the museum paperwork with her name in the "group leader" spot. She was pretty sure they'd be fine with it.

The teacher flipped through the stack of entries. "I'm thrilled to see that so many of you are entering the contest," she said. "And look at these ideas! There's some great thinking going on here. *Innovation: From the Model T to the Apple Computer. The Importance of Football, America's Favorite Pastime.*"

Football? Nadia thought. *Really?* In all her trips to the museum, she'd never seen a single thing about sports. Who had come up with that idea?

As if answering her thoughts, Jason fist-bumped Aiden and Mike.

"Good luck with that," Nadia muttered to herself.

The teacher continued. "*Suffragette City: Women's Fight for the Right to Vote.* And *Immigreat: A Look at Five Special American Citizens.*" Nadia smiled. She had worked hard on that title.

Ms. Arena looked up at the class. "I'm really proud of everyone who submitted entries. I can't wait to see your presentations!" She placed the forms in a manila envelope and asked a girl named Rebecca to deliver it to the main office. Some butterflies started up in Nadia's stomach. It was official—as Principal Taylor would say, now they were in it.

As if on cue, the loudspeaker crackled to life and Principal Taylor's voice rang out. "Good morning, Bridget Mason students! First of all, don't forget that the fall carnival is next weekend! Rides, games of chance, plus delicious and totally unhealthy food! I'm sad to say there won't be a trivia contest this year, but that's because we're going to have a . . . wait for it . . . DJ! That's right. Music by master DJ Ed U. Cator! Be there or be square!"

The class groaned. Principal Taylor could be so goofy sometimes.

"And I'm delighted to report that the museum exhibit entries are pouring into the office as I speak. Many thanks to all of you who are participating and representing Bridget Mason Middle School. May the best team win!"

"So I was thinking that even though the cash prize is very exciting, we should try to put it out of our minds," Nadia told everyone that day at lunch. It was a beautiful sunny day and they were sitting outside in the courtyard. "We just need to concentrate on creating a really amazing exhibit."

Vikram looked worried. "Do you think our idea is good enough?" he asked. "I mean, some of the ones my teacher read out in homeroom were pretty cool."

Adam shrugged. "Well, it's too late to change it now."

"Right," Nadia said. "But our idea is great. I mean, who doesn't like a good immigrant story?"

"Immigrants, huh?" said Jason, sitting down heavily and slinging his lunch bag onto the picnic table. "I knew that one was yours!"

Nadia frowned, uncomfortable with Jason's comment, but decided to let it slide. She opened her lunch bag instead. She was delighted to discover that Baba had packed her some fūl, a fava bean stew, with some pita bread to dip into it. She took a quick sniff. *So good.*

Jason was once again staring at her lunch, a disgusted

look on his face. *Rude,* she thought, but ignored him. He unwrapped his sandwich and took a big bite. "I just don't get it," he said through the mouthful of PB&J. "I mean, how are people from other countries American, you know?" He chewed and swallowed, then looked Nadia dead in the eye. "Let me guess. It was your idea, Ms. Egypt."

"Well, um . . ." Nadia started to say.

"It *was* your idea," said Adam.

Was she imagining things or did his voice sound almost accusatory all of a sudden?

Adam looked around the table at the Nerd Patrol. "Do you guys think we submitted a bad idea?"

"It's not as cool as football, that's for sure," said Jason, taking a sip of his chocolate milk.

Adam nodded. Nadia stared at him in disbelief.

"Um, hello," Chloe said to Jason, ignoring Adam's question. "America is a nation of immigrants. If you're not Native American, someone in your family was an immigrant. Or was enslaved and came here because someone made them."

Nadia turned from Adam to Chloe, surprised her friend had summed things up so easily.

"Yeah," Nadia added. "What Chloe said."

"Whatever," Jason scoffed. "I think we all know whose idea is coolest, and whose project is going to win."

Everyone looked at him as if to say, "We do?"

"Mine, of course!" Jason said.

Nadia raised her eyebrows. *Braggy, much?* Adam nodded as if to agree with Jason but stopped when he saw Nadia's expression. Everyone else busied themselves with their lunches. It was . . . awkward.

"Hey, what did the Chinese man say to the other Chinese man?" Jason finally said.

"I don't know," said Adam, his eyes brightening at the setup of another of Jason's jokes.

"Tell us!" said Vikram.

"How am I supposed to know?" said Jason. "I don't speak Chinese!"

Everyone burst out laughing, including Nadia. But then she bit the inside of her cheek to stop herself. Was she even supposed to find that amusing? Was it offensive? She wasn't quite sure. *Molten monkey muffins*, as Titi might say. Why was Jason so annoyingly funny?

Jason rushed off after he finished his lunch, and the conversation turned back to the project.

"So what do we need to do next, Nadia?" Chloe asked.

Oh, right, Nadia thought, popping the last of her pita bread in her mouth. She was group leader—her friends would be looking to her to make decisions and have a plan.

"Hmm . . ." she said. "Let's work separately on our

immigrant stories this week. Then there's that all-day Project Party at the museum on Saturday. We can figure out our creative presentation idea then."

Vikram, Chloe, and Sarah nodded, but Adam was staring off into space. "Adam?" Nadia said. "You okay?"

"Huh? Oh yeah," Adam said. "Saturday, project, museum. Got it."

Nadia stared at her friend. She wasn't sure what was going on with Adam, but he clearly needed some cheering up. She glanced around and saw a poster for the fall carnival.

"Hey!" she said. "We should all go to the carnival together after the Project Party! Play some games like the milk bottle toss." She snagged Adam's balled-up lunch sack and tossed it at his empty milk carton, which toppled over. "Though it's a bummer there's no trivia contest this year."

Adam and the rest of her friends broke into big grins at the mention of the carnival. Last year's was the first activity they had done together as a group. They had entered the trivia contest and chosen Nerd Patrol as their group name. They had won (of course), and the rest was history.

"Awesome," Adam said. "It's a plan!"

The rest of the day was busy, and Nadia didn't get a chance to see Titi until after dinner. Once everyone had finished eating and the dishwasher had been stacked, she was finally able to go upstairs to her room. She opened the door and dropped her backpack to the floor with a heavy sigh.

"Help," she said, and grabbed for the amulet . . . but her fingers came up empty!

She panicked for a moment before realizing she'd never put it back on after her shower that morning. (Not-so-fun fact: Two-thousand-year-old artifacts don't exactly react well to bubble-gum-scented shower gel.) She rescued the hippo from the bathroom counter. "Help!" she said again.

"Long day, huh?" Titi called. It took a moment for Nadia to find him on the wall calendar. "Not that I would know how it went," Titi continued, "since *someone* left me behind."

"Sorry," Nadia said. "It *was* a long day." She walked over to the bed and collapsed onto it.

"Hey!" called Titi. "I can't believe you didn't notice! Especially after all that fashion hullabaloo with Adam on the first day of school."

"Notice what?" said Nadia, sitting up.

"My new outfit!" said Titi, spinning around and striking a pose. "It's my latest power. I can finally change my clothes!" He was wearing an elegant suit, crisp white shirt, bright red power tie, and shiny shoes.

Nadia smiled. "I must admit, you do look snazzy."

"Watch this!" Titi exclaimed. "Cowboy! Athlete! Punk rocker! Scary clown! Lunch lady! Isn't it amazing?"

Nadia watched, her mouth slightly ajar, as Titi went through half a dozen outfit changes right before her eyes.

"Yeah, cool," she said. "I mean, I think? Do the clothes come with special powers to help me with my solutions?"

"Holy hippos, Nadia," said Titi with a wag of his finger. "Not *everything* is about you. This is the best power ever. I've been wearing that linen ensemble for two millennia!"

He snapped his fingers and settled on a white bedazzled jumpsuit with sunglasses and a towering black pompadour hairstyle.

"Well, hello there, Mr. Presley," said Nadia, giggling. "Hey, did you know Elvis recorded six hundred songs during his career, but he didn't write any of them?"

Titi jumped to a folder sitting on Nadia's desk. "I did not know that," he said. "But—and I know you've been waiting for this—enough about me. Tell me how the *EGYPTIAN EXTRAVAGANZA!* is coming along."

Nadia sighed. Though lunch had ended on a good note, she couldn't help but replay the awkward way it started off, particularly the part of the conversation where Jason said people from other countries weren't American. She knew that wasn't true. So why did it bother her so much? And Adam had almost seemed to agree with him . . .

"Ugh," Nadia said. "More like EXTRAVAGANTLY UNCOMFORTABLE. Not everyone is . . . confident in the idea. And Adam's acting weird, especially around the new kid."

"I'm all shook up!" Titi said. "Tell me more. Maybe I can help."

Nadia hesitated for a moment. The tiny teacher seemed good at school-like stuff. Math, history. But friend—or frenemy—stuff? Nadia wasn't so sure she trusted him with that kind of thing. "It . . . it's not important," she said.

"Try me," said Titi.

Nadia stared at the ceiling for a moment, then glanced at her bobbleheads. Normally she'd talk through stuff like this with them, but they never had any actual answers. What did she have to lose by talking to Titi?

So she filled Titi in on Jason, and before she knew it, she'd told him everything—how he was funny but seemed to hate everything about her. "He makes fun of my facts, and my Egyptian-ness—anything Egyptian— and my food." Nadia stopped, her voice cracking. For some reason, Jason making fun of the food her parents made her hurt the most of all. She grabbed the scarab-shaped pillow she'd gotten this summer and buried her face in it.

"Hold on," Titi said. He hopped from the folder to a book cover on her nightstand. "I've heard him make fun of your food and stuff. But Jason hates everything Egyptian? Does he hate mathematics? Paper? Toothpaste? How do you know? Does he have gingivitis? Yuck."

Nadia came out from behind the pillow to shoot Titi a look. "Is this supposed to be helping?"

"Sorry," Titi said. "It's just . . . I don't think this kid hates you because you are Egyptian. He focuses on that because it's one thing that makes you different. It's an easy way to get under your skin."

Nadia sat up. Jason had called Sarah "four-eyes" behind her back the other day because of her glasses. And he'd made fun of Oona's new shoes yesterday. "So it's not just me," Nadia said. "I get that. And I get that my Egyptian heritage is sort of"—she grabbed the amulet—"obvious, and that's why he makes fun of it. But . . ." Nadia lay back down with a sigh. "I *am* Egyptian—I can't change that. Jason is just going to keep teasing me."

"Exactly," Titi said. He made himself comfortable on the book cover. "This is not a new problem. People like Jason—bullies—have been around forever. This is *classic* Nemtynakht."

"Classic Nem-what?!" Nadia said.

"NEM-TEE-NAKT," Titi said. "Hold up! Miss Did-You-Know doesn't know the Egyptian parable of 'The Eloquent Peasant'?!"

"All right," Nadia said. "No need to get snarky. It does sound familiar. Just help me out with the details."

"Help you out? Is that a call for the fourth solution? Woo-hoo!" Titi did a flip. "I can have some fun with this. Let's go!"

"Go where?" Nadia said. But the WHOOSH drowned out her words. She was falling, falling, falling again. At least

IN ALL, THE PHARAOH HAD KHUN-ANUP PLEAD HIS CASE EIGHT MORE TIMES. AND EACH TIME THE PEASANT'S WORDS WERE DIFFERENT, BUT THEY WERE ALWAYS STRONG, AND POWERFUL, AND JUST. A SCRIBE RECORDED THEM ALL.

this time she was prepared for the drop onto the hot sand.

"I don't think I'll ever get used to that," said Nadia from her bedroom rug. It felt good to be standing on two legs again instead of four.

"So what do you think?" asked Titi. He was now on the kitten poster. "About Nemtynakht?"

"He was a bully, all right," Nadia said. "Big-time. But Khun-Anup—he was a freakin' superhero." She jumped up on her bed and struck a power pose. "Nemtynakht thought he was big and bad but Khun-Anup was like, 'You doofus. You stole my stuff, but I still have my words!' And Nemtynakht ended up looking like a fool."

"Yup," Titi said. "Nemtynakht helped himself to power but Khun-Anup took it right back." He pointed at Nadia. "Just like you can do with Jason."

Nadia plopped down on the bed. "Oh," she said. "I see what you did there. Clever."

"So you're good?" Titi said. "About Jason, I mean. 'Cause I think I need to go back into the amulet for a nap. Being a donkey is hard work."

Nadia nodded, then opened up the book on her nightstand. Titi jumped inside and struck his pose.

"To the hippo and beyond!" they said together as Nadia closed the book.

Once Titi disappeared, Nadia sat down at her desk.

Take the power back from Jason.

She could do that. She just had to figure out how.

Chapter Seven

Saturday morning, Nadia said a quick goodbye to her parents, grabbed a banana from the kitchen, and set off for Adam's house, where she was grabbing a ride to the museum. The weather matched her mood—bright and sunny. Last night, she and Titi had come up with the perfect idea for how to present their exhibit. But even better, Jason hadn't made fun of her all week. She had psyched herself up to take away his power Khun-Anup style, but Jason hadn't given her the opportunity. Maybe he'd been hit in the head with a basketball and it somehow knocked some sense into him.

Adam's stepdad was in the driver's seat. Nadia slid into the back seat next to Adam.

"Hey, Adam, Mr. Mayer," she said as she got into the car.

"Good morning, Natalie," said Adam's stepdad.

"Nadia," she and Adam said in unison.

"Oh, right," he said. "And you can call me Charlie."

"Gotcha," Nadia said. "Hey! Did you know that Charlie Chaplin once—" But Adam's stepdad had already turned on the radio. Two guys were discussing an upcoming game. Very loudly.

Adam shrugged and they rode the rest of the way in silence.

Nadia felt a little thrill of excitement when they walked up the steep stone steps leading to the museum entrance. There were important, historic things inside this old building. Tattered flags and military uniforms from long-ago wars. Letters written by US presidents and a spike from the Transcontinental Railroad. The exhibits were all carefully planned out to be informative and interesting and cool-looking. And to think—in just one week's time, the Nerd Patrol could have an exhibit among them!

No, Nadia corrected herself. *The Nerd Patrol will have an exhibit among them, because we are going to WIN.*

They checked in with the front desk and were directed up a staircase to a cordoned-off hallway.

"You'll see a sign that says 'Staff Only,'" the front desk employee told them, "but go on through."

Nadia's stomach did a little flip. "Awesome," she whispered to herself.

Their footsteps echoed as they walked down the empty hallway. The floors and walls were polished marble. Small carvings of eagles decorated the molding near the ceiling. (Fun fact: They were left over from when the museum building was the town's city hall.)

At the end of the hallway, the door to the special room was wide open, so Nadia and Adam strode right in. An older woman in a brown cardigan was seated at a table, reviewing some paperwork.

"Good morning!" Nadia said, so excited she was practically bursting. "Did you know that this museum was built in 1903, on the grounds of the town's original city hall?"

The woman jumped at the sound of Nadia's voice.

"Oh my Darjeeling!" she cried.

At first Nadia thought it was a genteel expression of surprise, but she quickly realized the woman had knocked over her Darjeeling tea. The woman tried to mop it off the desk with a single, sodden tissue.

"Um, I'll go get some paper towels," said Adam.

"Oh, thank you, dear," the woman said. She grabbed a clipboard, which had luckily escaped the tea. "My name is Ms. Gilson and I am the proctor for this project." She looked over her glasses at Nadia. "And you are?"

"Nadia Youssef." She offered her hand for a handshake.

Ms. Gilson shook it, then made a check next to Nadia's name. "Nadia—yes. I have a note here for you. The committee liked your group's idea, but because of time constraints on the day of the presentations, they requested that you put a special focus on one of your immigrants. The others can each have a shorter entry."

"Oh," said Nadia. Was this one of those times she should make a decision as group leader? She had already finished her immigrant report and it was pretty long. As of yesterday, Adam hadn't even decided on his immigrant. And Sarah and Chloe and Vikram hadn't finished theirs. "Okay, we'll put the focus on the Egyptian immigrant, Dr. Wafaa El-Sadr," she decided. Nadia was proud of her choice. Dr. El-Sadr devoted her life to the care and treatment of those with AIDS.

Ms. Gilson made a note on her clipboard. "Very well," she said.

Adam returned with the paper towels and they mopped up the tea. Then Ms. Gilson showed them around. "Pick a table," she told them. "It will belong to your group until the presentation. You can leave your projects here and they'll be perfectly safe. And over here"—she led them to an area in the back of the room—"are all the materials you have to work with."

Nadia was delighted to find boxes of all shapes and

sizes, poster board, tons of paper, paints, brushes, glue, markers, colored pencils, glue guns, wood, hammers and nails, needles, thread, bolts of fabric, and lots of other materials.

She and Adam found a table near the window as other students began to file in. Vikram was the first of their group to arrive.

"Morning, Nadia, Adam," Vikram said, giving them high fives.

Sarah and Chloe showed up a moment later and grabbed seats, too.

They all looked at Nadia expectantly. "So," Nadia began, "that woman Ms. Gilson was just telling me that we need to keep our presentation short. She suggested we focus on just one immigrant. So get this—your immigrant bios can be much shorter—maybe just half a page or so."

"Our bios?" Adam asked. "What about yours?"

"Yeah, what do you mean?" Sarah added.

Nadia shifted in her chair. This was supposed to be good news. "Well, I figured since I'm already done writing, mine could be the long one."

Chloe frowned. "But I finished mine, too. How come you made that decision without us?"

Nadia was taken aback. "Because—because I'm group leader. I thought that was my job?"

Adam frowned. "Your job is to keep us on track,

not decide how things go without asking us."

"Oh," Nadia said, a little lump forming in her throat. "Sorry, I just thought it would make everyone's lives easier."

Vikram shrugged. "I haven't written my part yet. But still, not cool, Nadia."

Nadia swallowed. *Point taken.*

There were an awkward few moments of silence. Nadia opened up her notebook as Adam drummed his fingers on the table.

"So we're supposed to figure out how to present to the museum board today, right?" Chloe finally asked. She looked to Nadia.

Nadia glanced from Chloe to Sarah to Adam to Vikram. Everyone seemed to expect her to answer. This leader stuff was *confusing.*

"Um, yeah," Nadia said. She pointed to the back of the room. "Those are the materials we have to work with. But I . . . I actually already have an idea—"

"I'm going to check out the materials," Sarah said, popping up from her chair. The others followed and suddenly Nadia was left alone at the table.

She grabbed her amulet out of habit. Today was not going as planned. She needed to break the tension in the room. And she herself was feeling a bit . . . shook up. She smiled, thinking of Titi Presley and his giant wall of hair.

Nadia found the proctor. "Ms. Gilson? Do you think we could put on some music, to liven up the mood in here? It's a Project Party after all, right?" The proctor didn't look convinced. Nadia pulled out her phone and turned to a streaming station, taking a wild guess at the older lady's tastes. "Maybe some . . . Elvis?" She pressed play and "Blue Suede Shoes" came on.

Ms. Gilson couldn't help but smile. "All right," she said. "Just not too loud."

Vikram returned to the table first. "I like it," he said, swiveling his hips.

"You put the music on?" Chloe said. "Good idea, Nadia."

The others agreed and Nadia breathed a sigh of relief.

"Speaking of good ideas, I have one for the presentation," Sarah said. She held up a wooden box. "What if we did a diorama? It could be a mini version of exactly the way we envision the exhibit will look. You know, photographs, and text, and artifacts. Think of all the cool miniatures we could make!" Sarah loved miniatures and collected them the way Nadia collected bobbleheads.

But Nadia shook her head. "No offense, Sarah, but that's just too small," she said. "We need to think big—"

"Exactly!" Chloe said. "So Adam and I came up with the idea to make a giant book. You know, like the ginormous ones the teachers used to read to the whole class when we were little."

Giant book, Nadia wrote down. *It's not as good as my idea*, she thought, but—

POOF! Suddenly, Titi appeared in her notebook in his full Elvis getup. Nadia's eyes went wide and she dove to cover him up, her head and arms on her notebook.

"Do I hear some Elvis tunes?" Titi said in a soft, muffled voice. "I thought maybe I could entertain your group with a lip sync, since I already have the outfit and all."

Nadia's mind raced. Had she said *help* while holding the amulet? What was Titi doing here?

"Um, Nadia?" Sarah tapped her on the shoulder and leaned in to see what Nadia was hiding. "Are you okay? Is that an idea for our project?"

Nadia peeked at Titi. He was frozen on the paper. At least he had that much sense. Nadia cautiously sat up.

"N-no," Nadia said. "It's just something I was doodling."

"Weird doodle," Sarah said, eyeing the page. "Since when are you so into Elvis?"

"I'm—I'm not," Nadia answered. "I just—"

"Can we focus here?" Adam said. "Our presentation? Giant book idea?"

"Oh yeah," Nadia said. "Go on."

But as Adam started talking, a bead of sweat appeared on Titi's forehead, from holding his awkward Elvis pose, Nadia figured. Nadia stood up, interrupting Adam.

"I . . . I'll be right back," she said. She grabbed her notebook and dashed into the hallway.

"Titi! What are you doing here?" she said as soon as the door was closed behind her.

Titi was now dressed like Indiana Jones, in a fedora, leather jacket, and khakis. He lifted the edge of his hat with the handle of the whip he was holding. "Guess who found out his new power?" he said with a wink.

"No more need for me to hold the hippo amulet and say help?" Nadia guessed.

He smiled broadly. "I can come and go as I please now," he said. "Isn't that fantastic?"

"That's one word for it," said Nadia.

"I'm here to see how the Egyptian Extravaganza is going." He unfurled the whip and drew it back to crack it. Unfortunately, it somehow got wrapped around his legs and he crashed to the ground, losing his hat in the process.

"I meant to do that," said Titi, unwrapping himself. Nadia just rolled her eyes.

"The project is going . . ." She paused. It certainly wasn't going great. "Fine. It was going fine until you showed up," she said. "Listen, if you're going to pop up whenever you please, we have to make some ground rules. You have to be discreet—no popping up when I'm sitting two feet from my friends."

"Okay, okay," Titi said. "I get it. Keep under the radar. Your friends aren't ready for this fabulousness anyway." He snapped his whip again and managed to stay on his feet this time.

Nadia rolled her eyes again.

Titi smiled sheepishly. "Sorry I threw you off your game. Now get back in there and show 'em what you've got. You're going to share that awesome idea for the presentation, right?"

Nadia nodded. She better get back inside, before her group went with a different idea. She waved to Titi, then gently closed her notebook.

Back inside, Vikram was sharing an idea. Nadia slid back into her seat.

"We need to think bold. Original. Attention getting." He looked around at everyone and then dramatically pulled a microphone out from under the table. He jumped up and stood on his chair, then sang his idea into the microphone. "I think we need to do a musicaaaaal!"

"Shhhhhh!" said Ms. Gilson. She was starting to look annoyed with their table.

"Vikram's right," Nadia said.

"You like the musical idea?" Vikram said excitedly,

hopping back down. "I already wrote some lyrics for my immigrant." He cleared his throat and began to sing—more quietly this time—to the tune of "I've Been Working on the Railroad."

I was working on the space shuttle

Kalpana Chawla was my name

I was the first Indian woman in space

The robotic arm's my claim to fame—"

"Actually," Nadia said, cutting him off. "I was thinking . . . What if we did a musical, just without the music?"

"You mean a play?" Sarah asked. Vikram frowned.

"Sort of," said Nadia. "Remember when my parents took me to Disneyland last spring break?" She turned to Adam, who was staring down at the table. Was he even listening?

Whatever, Nadia thought, glancing at the clock. They had to decide on an idea and get started working. She continued.

"My dad really wanted to go to the Hall of Presidents. I was all set for it to be lame, but the whole animatronic thing was actually kind of cool. I was thinking we could dress up like our characters and then pretend we're animatronic. Move like robots, you know?" She demonstrated by turning and moving her arms slowly. "Like when it starts we're all standing totally still while there's patriotic music playing and an

87

introduction that we recorded that tells all about how important immigrants have been to the history of the United States. And then, one by one, we start speaking and telling our stories."

Vikram frowned. "That's not as fun as a musical."

"Hmm. It would make us stand out from the other groups, I'll give you that," Chloe said. "What do you think, Adam?"

Adam shrugged.

SLAM!

The door flew open and a bunch of boys walked in, laughing and pushing one another. To her dismay, Nadia saw that it was Jason, Aiden, and Mike. Aiden was holding a football under his arm. Jason walked to the other side of the room. "Yo, Aiden!" he called. "Over here!"

Nadia gasped. "You can't toss a football in a museum!" she said.

"But you can play Elvis music?" said Adam. "Calm down, Grandma. Ms. Gilson is shutting it down."

Ms. Gilson hurried over and ushered the boys to a table. Nadia was pleased that it was on the other side of the room. And that the proctor confiscated their football.

"They may need that," said Adam worriedly. "For their project. It's about football, you know."

"I know," said Nadia. *Dumbest idea ever.* She turned back to her group.

"So are we all set with the animatronic idea?" Nadia

asked. "We'll need costumes. Makeup. Wigs. We'll have to write scripts. And props, we'll need props."

"Wait a minute," said Sarah. "We should vote on it. Chloe, what do you think?"

"If we're not going to do the giant book, the animatronic thing sounds okay," Chloe said.

"I maintain that the musical is still the best," Vikram said. "But maybe my robot can sing?"

"Sure," Nadia said, laughing.

"Making costumes sounds sort of fun," Sarah said. "Adam? Are you on board?"

Adam sighed. "The animatronic thing is fine. But I have an idea to make our presentation even shorter: I don't have to have my own immigrant. I can just help you guys with yours."

Nadia frowned. "Are you sure?"

Adam nodded. "I'm sure."

There was a knot forming in Nadia's stomach. She hated that her BFF wasn't into this when she was so excited. She knew the others weren't 100 percent in on her idea, either. But her gut told her it would be awesome. Baba was always saying that when you're unsure about something, get started and go from there. They just needed to get started.

"So we're set, then," Nadia said. She glanced at the clock. "We have five and a half hours to make our costumes and props. On your mark, get set, go!"

❖ ❖ ❖

"What do you think?" Vikram said five hours later. "Is it worthy of a singing robot astronaut?" He slipped the astronaut helmet he'd made out of tinfoil and cardboard over his head. Then he did a little jig as he sang his song about Kalpana Chawla.

Adam laughed. "You could be one of Nadia's bobbleheads in that thing!"

The last several hours had been great messy fun all around. Titi had shown back up but had been remarkably well behaved, just watching from the notebook cover (this time in a more relaxed position); Jason's group minded their own business; the pizza lunch was delicious; and Adam was in a much better mood—he'd even downloaded music for each of their parts and started working on a PowerPoint that would project images behind them as they presented.

"Your astronaut helmet is impressive," Nadia said to Vikram, "but check this out!" She turned her back to her friends and put on her own costume—a doctor's lab coat made from an extra-large men's dress shirt and a stethoscope made from a balloon, a plastic cap, some tubing, and some wire. Then she grabbed her poster. It had an infographic about Dr. El-Sadr's research on it . . . and about four jars' worth of glitter. "Presenting . . ." She flipped around to her friends and held the sign up. "Dr. Wafaa El-Sadr!"

"Wow—you look GREAT!" Sarah said. "I don't want to jinx it, but I think we could maybe win based on our costumes alone!"

Satisfied with their progress, the Nerd Patrol left their things on the table—they were going to come back Monday afternoon to put on the final touches—and headed outside.

"Nerd-Pa-trol. Ro-bots-for-the-win," Vikram said in a robot voice as they made their way down the stairs. "We're gonna rock this."

"Yeah we are!" Nadia said. *See? All we had to do was get started.*

"But first," Chloe added as they exited the building, "we've got some games of chance to conquer. Meet you all at the carnival entrance at eight o'clock?"

"Aff-ir-ma-tive," said Vikram. "Be-there. Or-be-square."

Chapter Eight

Corn dogs, funnel cakes, rides, games of chance," said Sarah, stating her preferred order of events.

Bridget Mason Middle School went all out for their yearly carnival. The field behind the school was filled with booths and real carnival rides and tons of food stands. Music filled the air as students, siblings, parents, and teachers wandered around with balloon strings and cotton candy cones clutched in their fists. Dusk was starting to fall and the lights of the rides, the food stands, and the midway were glowing, bright and cheerful. Nadia couldn't help grinning at the festive party atmosphere.

Chloe shook her head at Sarah. "Corn dogs and funnel cakes *after* the rides," she said. "We don't want a replay of last year when Vikram threw up after we went on the Tilt-A-Whirl, do we?"

"We certainly do not," said Vikram.

"Should we start with some games?" suggested Adam.

"To the games of chance!" shouted Sarah. The friends took off toward the midway, where the games and rides were. Nadia could see the Ferris wheel towering above the carnival in the distance.

"Did you know the Ferris wheel is named after the engineer who built the ride for the 1893 Chicago World's Fair?" Nadia called to her friends as they ran. "He only made the one, but they've all been called Ferris wheels ever since."

"Did you know I'm going to kick your butt at Whac-A-Mole?" Sarah shot back. Nadia laughed.

After trying to hit frogs onto lily pads with mallets, whack moles, toss rings, shoot baskets, and knock down stacks of milk bottles, all they had won among the five of them was a lame back scratcher.

Sarah sighed. "It's just not the carnival until one of us wins a stuffed animal."

Nadia pointed to a nearby game, which was deserted but had a ton of stuffed animal prizes. "Hey!" she said. "There's always a winner in the water gun game. If it's just the five of us competing, then one of us is guaranteed to win!"

"Great idea!" said Vikram. The friends ran over, slapped down their dollars, and each grabbed a water gun. Nadia stared at the clown, waiting for the starting bell. RING-A-LING! She pressed the trigger and aimed right at the clown's open mouth. The balloon got bigger, bigger . . .

POP!

Nadia's balloon deflated. Who had won?

The barker reached up and handed a stuffed snake to the winner. Nadia leaned over to see who it was.

"You've got to be kidding me," she muttered.

It was Jason.

Sarah turned to Nadia and shrugged. "He joined in at the last minute."

Jason slung the yellow-and-green snake around his neck. "Better luck next time," he said with a smirk. "Hey, Nadia, maybe you can teach me how to be a snake charmer!" He mimicked playing a flute.

"Snake charmers are from India," corrected Vikram.

"Actually, the practice of snake charming originated in Egypt," Nadia said reluctantly. She hated to admit that Jason was right, even by mistake, but she couldn't help sharing this fun fact.

"Really?" said Vikram. "Our cultures meet again!" He bumped fists with Nadia.

"That's a really weird thing to fist-bump over, you know that?" said Jason. He laughed.

"Goodbye, Jason," Nadia said, turning her back on him. "Where to next?" she asked her friends. "Ferris wheel or . . ." She gave Vikram a glance. "Tilt-A-Whirl?"

"Let's start small," said Vikram, putting a hand to his stomach.

"The merry-go-round it is," she joked.

The friends headed toward the rides, Vikram in the lead. The music started getting louder as they walked. Nadia recognized the tune as one her parents listened to in the car—something about not worrying and being happy.

Suddenly, Vikram stopped short. Nadia slammed right into him, and Chloe right into her.

"Are you seeing what I'm seeing?" Vikram said.

Nadia peered over his shoulder. She saw an empty dance floor and a DJ table set up behind it. A big sign read DJ ED U. CATOR.

"Ed-U-Cator," said Chloe slowly. "DJ *Educator*. I can't believe we missed that during announcements. Is this a bad dream or is this really happening?"

The five friends stared in disbelief as their principal, dressed in an oversized hoodie, ripped jeans, and high-tops, spun records at a turntable. He was wearing a giant pair of headphones. "Hey, guys!" he shouted. "Can I spin you some tunes?"

Nadia tried to answer, but couldn't find the words.

Principal Taylor took off the headphones. "Sorry,

was I being too loud?" he said in a normal voice. "Any requests?"

"I've got one," said a familiar voice.

Jason strode up to the DJ table, leaned over, and whispered in the principal's ear.

"A classic!" said the principal. "I'll play it next."

The non-worried/happy song wound down as the next song began to play. DJ Ed U. Cator was actually pretty smooth, Nadia had to give him that.

But she groaned when she recognized the new tune. It was that old-school pop song "Walk Like an Egyptian" by the Bangles. Some people in her extended family were offended by it. Others thought it was silly but fun. Nadia fell somewhere in the middle—she and her cousins had choreographed a dance to it one rainy afternoon that summer, but it's not like she would choose the song at karaoke.

Jason thinks he's so funny, Nadia thought. But she was surprised Principal Taylor would play a song like that. Would he play a song called "Walk Like an Italian"? Or "Walk Like a Native American"? Nadia didn't think so.

"This should be interesting," Nadia muttered to herself, a knot of dread forming in her stomach.

She bit her lip as Jason stepped onto the dance floor. He tossed the stuffed snake to one of his friends, then struck a pose—in profile, one arm raised in the front and the other in the back. It could have been the person

97

on the WALK/DON'T WALK signs, but Nadia knew better. He was imitating the way ancient Egyptians drew human figures. Nadia had seen them herself on the walls of royal tombs in Egypt. (Fun fact: Ancient Egyptians drew the figures like that on purpose, not because they didn't know how to draw.)

Jason took a couple of staggering steps forward with his arms in the awkward position. He moved his head forward and back like a pigeon, too, a huge grin on his face. Students were starting to gather, laughing with Jason and clapping along.

"Hey, Nadia, they're playing your song!" Jason shouted. "Am I doing it right? Is this how Egyptians walk?"

Several classmates howled with laughter as all eyes turned toward Nadia. Her face grew hot. She couldn't believe she'd actually thought Jason had maybe changed this week, that he was done making fun of her. She'd been so stupid.

"Well, Nadia?" Jason's buddy Aiden called out. "Are we doing it right?" He started doing the goofy dance, too, and a few classmates applauded. Next to Nadia, Adam let out a little laugh.

Nadia whipped her head around to glare at her friend, her blood boiling. But something else caught her eye.

Behind Adam's head, on a sign advertising corn

dogs, Titi was dressed in an Egyptian headdress, standing in the same pose as Jason. Nadia glanced around, but between Jason and Aiden and the bright lights of the carnival, no one else seemed to notice Titi.

POOF, Titi turned into Donkey Titi from the Khun-Anup parable, and winked. Nadia couldn't help herself—she let out a giggle.

She got Titi's message loud and clear: *Time to take away Jason's power.*

Nadia thought fast. She took a deep breath, grabbed the back scratcher from Chloe, and then strutted to the middle of the dance floor.

"Actually," she said loudly, "take it from a real Egyptian. This is how it's done." She held the back scratcher over her head and began to do a playful dance, bouncing from foot to foot. Then she kicked one leg out to the side, then the other. She and her cousins hadn't just choreographed their own dances this summer— they'd taken some Egyptian folk dancing classes, too. This one, her favorite, was performed using a cane as a baton.

Sarah and Chloe clapped delightedly. "Woo-hoo!" they shouted.

Next, Nadia began spinning the back scratcher like a majorette. She shimmied her shoulders, then jumped from one foot to the other.

"Oooohhhhh," Mike called out. "Girl got some moves!" The crowd roared.

"Go, Nadia!" shouted Vikram.

Jason stopped dancing, a confused look on his face.

"You're welcome to join me," Nadia said to Jason.

She danced around him, shaking her hips. Confused, he tried to move away from her and stumbled. Nadia turned her back on him and continued to work the crowd with her nimble moves. As the song wound to a close, she began to spin around, faster and faster. She was glad she had worn her new sequined skirt; it flared out perfectly and the sequins sparkled under the carnival lights. She felt like she was in a music video.

The crowded responded with cheers and applause. Nadia's cheeks hurt from smiling so big.

She did one last spin and came to a stop just as the song ended, dramatically tossing her head back so her hair flew up. She struck a pose with her arms stretched high, the back scratcher held triumphantly above her head.

The crowd exploded into cheers.

"Our very own Nadia Youssef, showing us how to walk . . . make that *dance* like an Egyptian!" announced Principal Taylor. "Thank you, Nadia, for teaching us how it's done!" The crowd cheered. He started another song, this one not from several decades ago, and kids started to make their way to the dance floor.

Nadia took a little bow, grinning from ear to ear.

As she straightened up, she caught a glimpse of Jason at the edge of the crowd, his face clouded over.

"Bro," Mike said as Jason grabbed back his stuffed snake, "she schooled you!"

Jason shoved his friend but didn't say anything else. Then he stormed off into the carnival crowd.

Nadia watched him go, then turned back to her friends on the dance floor.

"Teach us how to shake our hips like that!" Chloe said. Sarah wanted to learn, too.

So Nadia broke it down for them, but not without first glancing over at the corn dog poster and giving Titi a big thumbs-up.

Jason had officially been Khun-Anup'd.

Chapter Nine

Hey, Dancing Queen!"

Nadia was settling into her seat in homeroom on Monday when someone tapped her on the shoulder. It was her classmate Oona, though it took a moment for Nadia to recognize her. Oona was usually a quiet, fly-under-the-radar type of girl. But today, the ends of her curly hair were dyed fluorescent pink.

"I just wanted to say it was awesome when you stood up to Jason on Saturday," Oona said.

Nadia grinned. "Thanks, Oona. And I love the new hair color!"

"Me too!" Sarah said, slipping into her own seat. Oona walked away and Sarah turned to Nadia. "Where's Adam?"

"Not sure," Nadia said. "He texted that he was running late and I should go without him."

Nadia took the few minutes before the bell to reorganize her backpack. She was usually methodical about packing it, but this morning, she'd basically thrown the contents of her desk into it without even looking. As she rearranged her notebooks and textbooks by size, she found the comic book among them. She glanced over her shoulder, relieved to see that Adam hadn't arrived yet. She tucked the comic into the very back of her bag as the bell rang and Adam slid into his seat.

"Everything okay?" Nadia mouthed to Adam.

But Adam wasn't even looking at her. He was turned to the back of the room . . . and waving at Jason. *Seriously?!* Nadia thought. *After everything that happened at the carnival?!*

At least Jason didn't wave back at Adam. He saw him, but ignored him. *Good*, Nadia thought.

Just then, the loudspeaker clicked on.

"Good Monday morning to you, students!" Principal Taylor said. "I'm just popping up with two announcements. First: Thank you ALL for making our carnival an amazing success. And second: Remember that the presentations for the museum contest will be held this Saturday at the Museum of American History! Come support your classmates, and GOOD LUCK to the competitors! This is DJ Ed—I mean, Principal Taylor signing off. Have a super-duper day!"

Ding!

   Ding!

   Ding!

Nadia, Sarah, and Adam were in Mrs. Choi's car on the way to the museum after school when all three of their phones chimed. It was a group text from Vikram. He and Chloe had gone to the museum ahead of them.

💩 💩 💩 Project emergency! Hurry up!

They all looked at one another, eyes wide.

"Mom," Sarah said, "can you drive any faster?"

Five minutes later, they hopped out of the minivan and dashed inside. That ball of dread was back in Nadia's stomach, even bigger than it had been at the carnival. What could be so urgent?

They raced down the hall, turned into the project room, and came to a halt. Vikram was standing at the table cradling his astronaut helmet—or what used to be his astronaut helmet—in his arms, like a tinfoil baby. Chloe was dazedly sifting through a pile of fabric, paper, and glitter on the table.

Wait. Nadia recognized that glitter.

"My poster!" She ran over to the table. Her infographic was ripped into a dozen pieces. And there was the balloon for her stethoscope, but what about the wire, the cap?

She glanced around. Everything they had left behind on Saturday was still on the table . . . just totally, utterly destroyed.

Ms. Gilson came over, wringing her hands. "I'm so sorry," she said. "There's been a bit of . . . an accident. I left the room for a couple of minutes a bit earlier and when I returned . . ." She gestured to their table.

Sarah sat down and began to cry. Chloe put her head in her hands. Adam . . . well, he looked angry more than sad.

Nadia sat down, too; she was shaking. All their hard work—ruined. Who would do this? And why? She glanced around. Were any of the other projects destroyed?

"I'm so sorry," Ms. Gilson said again. "I have no idea how this could have happened. I'll let the museum directors know, but there's no security footage of this area."

"I'm pretty sure I know how it happened," said Nadia darkly. She stared at Jason's table, piled high with a cardboard goalpost, jerseys, and a football.

Adam followed her gaze. "No way. Jason jokes around, but he wouldn't destroy our project."

Nadia shook her head. Adam was seriously getting on her nerves these days. First his attitude about the project, now this.

"*Why* are you so determined to be Jason's friend?" Nadia said to Adam as Ms. Gilson walked away. "It's not worth it."

Adam stared at her like he was going to say something, then changed his mind.

Chloe let out a whine. "What are we going to do? There's no way we can remake all this by Saturday."

Nadia was wondering the same thing. She grabbed the amulet. Was there a way for Titi to help?

"Well, I don't think there's anything we can do about it today," said Sarah. "All the materials here are picked over. We'd have to start from scratch at home. I'm going to text my mom to come back and get us."

In silence, the group picked everything up off the table and trudged to the garbage bin, then headed downstairs to wait for their ride.

"Hey, everyone!" said Mrs. Choi cheerfully once everyone was buckled in. "That was quick. Are you all done with the project?"

Silence.

"Someone trashed our costumes and props," Vikram finally said.

"Oh, that's terrible," said Mrs. Choi. "I'm so sorry. The museum doesn't know who did it?"

More silence.

"I know," Mrs. Choi suddenly said. "I'm taking you to Ice Scream for a treat."

"Mom," Sarah started. "I don't think ice cream is going to fix—"

"No arguing," Mrs. Choi said. "Ice cream never hurts."

Nadia frowned. Ice cream was definitely not going to fix this. Could they fix this?

Mrs. Choi handed Sarah some cash for everyone's ice cream and dropped them off. Inside, they ordered their ice cream one by one. Nadia considered getting the same sundae she'd had with Adam a couple weeks ago, but in her current mood, such a big treat seemed overwhelming. She ordered a scoop of strawberry.

Vikram, on the other hand, seemed to want to drown his feelings in sugar. He ordered something called death by chocolate, a giant hot-fudge-covered concoction.

They picked a table in the corner and sat down. After a few more minutes of silence, Vikram spoke up.

"So what do we do from here? Do we turn Jason in? He shouldn't be able to get away with this."

Chloe shrugged. "Can we even prove it was him?"

"Even if it was Jason," Adam said quickly, "can you blame him after how Nadia embarrassed him at the carnival?"

Nadia froze with her spoon halfway to her mouth. "Adam, are you seriously on the side of that . . . bully, rather than your BFF?"

Adam squirmed in his seat, then looked Nadia in the eyes. "It's just . . . I know he singles you out, but it's not like he's ever called you a racist name or anything. What's the big deal?"

"What's the big deal?" Nadia said. "He constantly makes fun of me for my background. That is NOT okay." She dropped her spoon. "Not that you would understand that."

Adam flinched. "What's that supposed to mean?"

Nadia paused, surprised that comment had even come out of her mouth. Adam was white and she wasn't, but that fact had never come up before. Not once.

Vikram, Sarah, and Chloe had stopped eating and were staring at Adam and Nadia.

"It doesn't matter why Jason did it," Nadia said. "He destroyed our project. Our project. Or don't you even care about that anymore?"

"Maybe I don't," Adam said, shrugging. "But maybe I would have cared about the project more if you had actually listened to anyone else's ideas. You got up and left when I was talking on Saturday, Nadia. Do you know how rude that was?"

Nadia frowned again, trying to figure out what Adam was talking about. Then she remembered Titi's interruption at the museum. "It's . . . That was complicated."

"Whatever," Adam said. "You're just a big—"

"Hey, guys," Sarah said. "Maybe we should finish our ice cream and go home. Cool off, regroup tomorrow."

Nadia stabbed her ice cream with her spoon, not looking at anyone. Her eyes were starting to fill with tears. She stared hard at her ice cream, willing the tears to go away. When did things get so messed up with Adam?

The bell above the door jangled, jostling Nadia from her thoughts. A noisy group of boys staggered inside.

Perfect, Nadia thought. *As if this afternoon could get any worse.*

"Hey, Jason," Adam called out.

Jason glanced over and took in the scene, then sauntered over to their table. "Well, if it isn't the Egyptian Dancing Queen and her minions. Is this a group meeting for your project? How's it coming along anyway?" He smirked.

Nadia narrowed her eyes. That was as good as an admission of guilt as anything. She turned to Adam as if to say "See?" Adam looked from Nadia to Jason. "Jason," Adam said. "Did you . . . I mean, you weren't at the museum earlier this afternoon, were you?"

"Maybe I was, maybe I wasn't," Jason said with a shrug.

Adam's face fell.

"Why would you do that?" Vikram said to Jason, putting his sundae down on the table. "We worked hard on our project just like you guys."

"Jason, you want me to order you something?" Mike called out from over by the counter.

Jason shrugged again, in answer to both Vikram

and Mike. "How about a big scoop of She Got What She Deserved?" he said, staring at Nadia.

Nadia fumed, her heart beating hard.

"Um, I don't think they have that flavor," Mike called back.

"Idiot," Jason said. "It's a— Never mind. Just get me a scoop of chocolate chip. Or is there another *exotic* flavor I should try?" He looked around at everyone in the group (except Adam) as he said it.

Nadia knew she should hold it together, take Jason's power away and all that, but it was like all of Jason's comments over the last few weeks had slowly been building up inside her, getting higher and higher, and were now pushing against the top of her skull. It felt like her brain was about to explode. She had to let it out.

"What is wrong with you?" Nadia spat. She stood up. "How can you think it's okay to make fun of me because of where I come from? What century were you born in?"

"This one," Jason said, "unlike your people, who are ancient history. When are you going to get it? This is America. Nobody cares about stuff like that."

Nadia scowled. "Oh, because *your* project is so important. Football—it's just a *game*. You think the Museum of American History is going to do a whole exhibit about a stupid *game*?"

A look of hurt crossed Jason's face, but a moment later he laughed. "Ooooohhh, I've angered the Egyptian goddess. What are you going to do, use your weirdo necklace to cast a magic hex on me?"

"Something like that," Nadia heard herself say, her hands balling into fists. She'd never hit anyone before, but there was a first time for everything. She lunged at Jason . . . and tripped over her backpack.

Jason laughed, but as Nadia fell, she knocked into him and he lost his balance, falling backward onto the table.

SQUASH. Jason landed on Vikram's death-by-chocolate sundae. Everybody froze for a moment, then Jason jumped back off the table and took a look at his backside. So did everyone else.

"Oh man!" Mike said. "It looks like you pooped your pants!"

Nadia burst out laughing. So did all her friends.

"Shut up!" Jason said to Mike. "Get me some napkins. Now!"

Mike scrambled as everyone stared at Jason. Jason turned to Nadia, his eyes narrowed into slits of pure anger. "You," he said. "This is all your fault. Everywhere you go you mess everything up. You don't even belong here. Why don't you just go back where you came from?!"

Her friends gasped. Nadia just stood there. She was, for the first time she could remember, completely speechless.

"Hey!" Adam's voice broke the silence as he stepped up to Jason. "That's enough," he said. "You don't talk to my friend—or anyone—that way. Get out of here."

Nadia's face softened. That was the BFF she knew.

Jason opened his mouth to reply but then seemed to think better of it. He jerked his head toward Mike and Aiden. "Let's go." He pushed past Adam and started for the door. On the way, he kicked Nadia's backpack, sending the contents flying across the floor. The bells above the door jangled violently as the boys left.

Nadia let out a breath she didn't know she'd been holding. She felt an odd combination of emotions: furious with Jason and grateful to Adam for standing up for her.

"Thank you," she said to Adam, who was on the floor picking up her things.

Adam looked back over his shoulder, his brow furrowed. "Don't you mean to say *I'm sorry?*"

"What?" Nadia said, but froze when she saw what he was holding.

The comic.

"You lied to me. You had my present all along," Adam said. He thrust the comic in Nadia's face. "You're so . . . selfish. You kept this for yourself. You elected *yourself* project group leader. You made *your* immigrant the focus without asking any of us what we wanted to do. You picked *your* way to do the presentation." He threw the comic at her. "You're just a big know-it-all who does whatever you want."

Nadia stared at her best friend. Was that really what he thought?

But then a ball of anger grew in her chest.

"You're one to talk," she shot back. "You've had the worst attitude about the project almost from the start. Right, guys?"

She turned to her other friends, but they were silent.

Nadia quickly gathered up the comic and her backpack. "Fine. You all don't like my ideas for the project? Do whatever you want," she said. She marched toward the door. "Because I quit."

Chapter Ten

The lump in Nadia's throat grew larger as she strode toward home.

How did everything get so messed up? Her best friend thought she was selfish. Her other friends didn't stand up for her. Their project was ruined. *And Jason . . .*

This was all Jason's fault. Everything was fine until he came along. She could hardly bear to think about what he'd said to her. *Telling me to go back to Egypt . . .*

As she turned down her block, a new thought crossed her mind: *I wish I could go back to Egypt. Or better yet, I wish we never left in the first place. None of this would have happened if my family had never left Egypt. I'd be in sixth grade in Cairo right now. Everyone would bring Egyptian food for lunch . . .*

She paused for a moment. *Actually, if I lived in Egypt, it would just be called "food." And I'd probably have an awesome best friend, or at least one who didn't call me names . . .*

Nadia pushed open the front door to her house and stomped inside. She paused briefly to take—or more like rip—off her shoes. She threw the right one down in a huff.

Her father looked up from the couch, where he was reading the Egyptian news on his iPad, like every evening. "Nadia? What's the matter, habibti?" he asked.

Nadia pulled her left shoe but it wouldn't come off. "What's the matter? Everything! Everything is the matter. I wish we never left Egypt! Why did we have to leave Egypt?!" She gave her shoe one last yank.

Mama entered the room as Nadia threw that shoe down, too.

"Come here, my love," said her mother. "We can—"

But Nadia stormed past them and up the stairs. She slammed her bedroom door shut behind her, collapsed on her bed, and cried.

She cried long and hard, great gasping breaths. It felt good and bad in equal amounts. Nadia had needed to cry like that for some time, she realized.

Her parents knocked on her door, but she told them to go away.

A while later, when her tears finally dried up, a small voice sounded in her ear. Her puffy eyes popped open.

"Nadia?" Titi was staring at her from the comic book, which, she discovered, she was still clutching in her hand. His face was sad, like he was genuinely concerned for her. "Is there anything I can do? Can I offer any solutions?"

"Not now, Titi," Nadia said. "Leave me alone."

Wait. Nadia sat up.

It was Titi's idea to do the project on Egypt. It was his lesson in the comic book that led to the carnival incident. And it was his fault she hadn't given Adam the comic book in the first place.

Her parents had brought the family to America years ago. But none of the stuff over the last couple of weeks would have happened if it weren't for Titi. Nadia turned to her bobbleheads.

"I should have stuck with you guys," she said. "At least you never give me bad advice."

On the comic, Titi looked crushed. Nadia's heart tugged, but she knew deep down she should have stuck with facts instead of magic; facts never let her down.

"I hate to say it, Titi," Nadia said, "but you're one of my problems. The solution is for you to go away."

Titi froze, shocked by Nadia's words. Then he nodded. "If it will help you, then I will get lost," he said. "But you're sure you want to use your fifth solution for that?"

Nadia nodded. She needed all this to just . . . disappear. "I'm sure."

Titi sighed. "If you change your mind, hold the amulet and say the magic word, okay? Like old times? Goodbye, Nadia." And with a POOF, Titi was gone.

Nadia shoved the comic under her bed, then took off her hippo amulet and placed it on her nightstand.

She laid her head down on her pillow and fell fast asleep.

Chapter Eleven

Hey, what happened to your hippo necklace?" Oona asked Nadia at lunch. It was Wednesday afternoon, and Nadia had eaten lunch with Oona and her friends Andrew, Abby, and Ella yesterday, too. In fact, she hadn't spoken to anyone in the Nerd Patrol since she stormed out of Ice Scream on Monday.

"And you haven't been wearing any of your cool Egyptian stuff this week, either," Oona added, her pink curls piled on top of her head. "What's up with that?"

Nadia shrugged. She'd decided that it was best to not give Jason more opportunities to make fun of her than necessary, so she'd shoved all her Egyptian-inspired clothing to the back of her closet. Of course, she still looked "exotic" with her dark hair and skin, but there wasn't anything she could do about that. "I decided to save that stuff for special occasions," she told Oona.

"Is it true that Jason ruined your project?" Andrew asked.

Nadia sighed. "Yeah. He pretty much admitted to it."

"That's terrible," said Abby.

"After all your hard work," added Ella.

"It doesn't matter," said Nadia. "I'm not doing the project anymore."

"Oh. That's too bad," said Oona, looking sad. "I mean, there's less competition for us now. You always have such great ideas—we know your project was going to be awesome."

Yes, Nadia thought. *Exactly. My ideas are good.* Her friends had agreed, even. So why were they—Adam especially—so mad at her?

She wondered if she would ever talk to the Nerd Patrol again. Just yesterday, when Adam had turned around in class, she had been expecting an apology. But he was just passing her a handout, stony-faced.

"Did you hear that Jason's group changed their presentation?" said Ella. "I overheard Mike saying that they are totally freaking out about getting it done. It's not just football anymore."

Yippee, thought Nadia. *Just what everyone needs. More sports.*

Later that afternoon, Nadia sat down in Mr. Decker's social studies class and took out her notebook. She opened it to the last page she had written on.

Huh. *That's weird,* she thought. It was her handwriting, but the notes weren't organized the way she usually wrote them, with neat headers and bullet points and sub-bullet points. (Fact: Proper note-taking is key to acing Mr. Decker's tests.) Maybe all this friend stuff was throwing her off her game more than she thought. She looked closer . . . and realized these weren't her notes at all! It was a letter from Titi!

My dear Nadia,

I know you don't want to see me, but I figured out my new power and there's no one else to tell: I'M NO LONGER LIMITED TO ANCIENT EGYPT! I CAN TRAVEL TO ANY TIME AND ANY PLACE IN THE COMIC! How awesome is that?! Think of all the fun facts you could learn!

If you want to go for a dive, just say the magic word, okay? I'm here.

Your friend, Titi

PS-Pushing these letters around was HARD WORK.

PPS-But you do have very nice handwriting.

PPPS-I miss you.

c t a e t d
v y

Nadia sat back in her chair. Traveling to anywhere in history was seriously cool. But then she shook her head. Magic had brought her nothing but trouble. And now, thanks to magic, she was missing a page of her social studies notes. She tore the page out and crumpled it into a ball.

"So, class," Mr. Decker started. "Today we begin our unit on ancient Egypt. Egypt is considered a cradle of civilization because so many inventions from ancient Egypt shaped the world as it is today."

Nadia looked up. She knew they would be studying her home country's history at some point during the year, but she had no idea they would start today.

"Nadia, do you have anything to share about Egypt with the class before I start the lesson?" Mr. Decker looked at her eagerly.

"Oh," Nadia said. "Um . . ."

Mr. Decker grew flustered. "I—I—I'm sorry," he stammered. "I didn't mean to make you uncomfortable. And I'm just now realizing I assumed you were Egyptian based on your name and those awesome outfits you wear. But I shouldn't have assumed. Are you Egyptian? You don't have to answer if you don't want to."

Nadia stared back at her anxious teacher. She was Egyptian, of course, and certainly felt it these days, too much so, thanks to Jason. *How ironic that in Egypt*

I'm always "the American cousin," but here I seem to be "the Egyptian girl . . ." she thought.

Nadia sat up straighter. Jason wasn't in this class, and she had a million and one facts she could share. She took a deep breath.

"Did you know that ancient Egyptians were probably the first conservationists?" She went on to explain about the Book of the Dead and how it said that when a person died and was judged by the ancient gods, they had to swear to two things: that they had not lied, or cheated, or killed, or harmed others; and that they preserved the Nile River and kept it pure and never deprived animals from their grass or birds from their fish and didn't interfere in how the water ran its paths.

Mr. Decker smiled. "The ancient Egyptians truly were ahead of their time," he said. "What a fascinating culture. You must be really proud of where you come from. And we're grateful to have you here to share your culture with us. I'm sure it wasn't an easy choice for your family to leave everything behind and come here."

Nadia nodded, mostly to get Mr. Decker to stop talking, but as he began his lesson, she realized something: She had no idea why her parents left Egypt. *Was* it a hard choice? They both came from large families, but none of their relatives had come to the United

States. Why had her parents come to a country where they didn't know anyone?

Ever since Nadia had come home upset on Monday, her parents had been trying to find out what was wrong. But she told them she didn't want to talk about it. She'd been so busy being mad at them for bringing her here, she'd never thought about why they'd come. Maybe it was time to find out.

"Baba? Mama?" Nadia said at dinner that night. "Why did we come to America?"

Baba paused with the serving spoon halfway to his plate. "That's a big question, habibti. It's complicated. Does this have something to do with the other night? All that about wishing we weren't in the US?"

Nadia hung her head, but nodded. "I want to know why we came here. Can you try to explain it?"

Her parents exchanged a glance.

"Okay, habibti, we will try," said Mama.

Nadia put her fork down. Her mom had made a delicious stew called molokhia. It was one of Nadia's favorites, but she wanted to give this conversation her undivided attention.

"When you were a baby," Baba began, "there was an uprising to bring democracy to the Middle East and Northern Africa. It was called the Arab Spring. After years of corruption in the Egyptian government, the ruler, a dictator named Mubarak, was overthrown. Mama and I took part in it. We brought food to the protesters and treated their injuries."

"We fought for years for a better Egypt," Mama explained. "And things did change. At least for a while. We had high hopes for the future. But sadly, it was just more of the same. People who opposed the government were still being imprisoned, and tortured, and killed. We realized we did not want to raise you in that kind of environment."

"And we had been identified as troublemakers," Baba continued. "It was too dangerous for us to stay. So we left our family and friends and made a new life here with you."

Wow. Nadia stared at both her parents, wide-eyed. "How did I not know any of this before now?"

"It was a scary time," said Mama. "We don't talk about it very much. But you are right; now you are old enough to fully understand."

"It must have been so hard to leave everyone you loved behind and start over completely," Nadia said.

"It *was* hard," said Baba. "But we wanted the best and safest life for you. In a place where everyone can speak their mind, without fear." He took a sip of water. "But where is all this coming from?"

Nadia twisted her napkin in her lap. And then she told her parents everything that had happened with Jason.

"Is that why you took off your amulet?" Mama asked when Nadia was done.

Nadia went to grab for it out of habit, but of course it wasn't there. She nodded.

"We're so sorry you've had to deal with this," Baba said.

"I wish you had told us sooner," added Mama. "Baba and I have had our share of unpleasant situations

ourselves, like when another Egyptian family moved into the neighborhood. A cashier at the supermarket told me that 'my people were taking over the town.'"

Baba told Nadia about the nervous looks he often got at the airport from other passengers.

And the extra security checks he was "randomly" subject to.

Nadia shook her head as she picked her fork back up. "Why do people think that's okay?"

"People are afraid of what they don't know," Baba said. "Maybe Jason didn't meet a lot of people from different backgrounds where he used to live. Or maybe his parents are narrow-minded and he gets his attitude from them."

Nadia stopped mid-bite. "You're defending him? Are you saying I should let him off the hook?" Maybe talking to her parents wasn't a good idea after all.

"No, of course not, but he may not know any different," Mama said. She helped herself to more molokhia. "Or he may think that because someone is not the same as him, it might mean they are better than him, so he puts you down to make sure you—and others—don't start to think that. He may not even know he's doing it."

Nadia nodded. That was classic Nemtynakht.

"But what am I supposed to do about it?" Nadia said. "Everything I've tried so far has backfired. And it's not my fault he doesn't know any better."

"That's exactly right, Nadia," said Baba. "It's not your job to teach him a lesson. But he can learn a lot from you."

"I'll share a secret," Mama said. "I've found that the best way to get through to people like Jason is to let them get to know you. That cashier at the supermarket? She saw me with you one time and told me she has a daughter the same age. We chat about you girls now—"

"What?!" Nadia said. "You talk about me with a random cashier?! That's weird, Mama!"

Mama laughed. "It's something we have in common. It showed her that we aren't so different after all. And now sometimes she asks what dish I'm cooking when I buy ingredients. Getting to know me has allowed her view to shift."

"I know it's not easy, *habibti*," Baba said. He got up and put his arm around Nadia. "But you can't let him stop you from being you, from doing what's important to you."

"Speaking of . . ." Mama said. "How's that project coming along for the museum? It's coming up soon, isn't it? You're welcome to have your friends over to work on it some more."

Nadia bit her lip. "It . . . it's complicated," she said. She wasn't quite sure what to say.

But she did know one thing: That contest was important to her. And she wasn't going to let Jason—or anyone—keep her from winning.

"May I be excused?" Nadia asked.

Upstairs, she typed out a group text.

Calling all Nerds! Can we meet at my locker in the a.m.? I need to talk to you.

She took a deep breath and pressed the send button. Then she put her phone down and stared at it, willing it to chime.

Ding! **Yeah.** Vikram was the first to respond.

Ding! **Um ... sure**, Chloe replied next.

Ding! **Okay**, Sarah texted.

Nadia smiled each time her phone chimed. She waited for the final reply, but an hour later, Adam still hadn't responded.

"Well," she said to her bobbleheads, "three out of four is a start."

Chapter Twelve

Nadia was so nervous, she woke up extra early. She got dressed, then swung her backpack onto her shoulder.

PLOP. Her backpack knocked something from her nightstand onto the floor. The amulet.

As Nadia picked it up, she flashed back to seeing the hippo for the first time at the Egyptian bazaar. The necklace felt good in her hand just like it had that day.

She held it up in front of the mirror. Titi or no Titi, she just felt more like herself while wearing the hippo. She fastened it around her neck and turned to her Amelia Earhart bobblehead.

"I'll just have to remember not to say hel—I

mean, the magic word—while holding it, right?"

Amelia nodded.

"So, um, thanks for meeting me," Nadia said. She, Sarah, Chloe, and Vikram were huddled in front of her locker. Adam was down the hall. He'd glanced their way as he'd passed, but had continued walking.

Nadia grabbed the hippo nervously. "Can I ask you something?" she said to her friends. "What Adam said at Ice Scream—did I take over the project?"

Her three friends exchanged glances. Sarah finally spoke up. "Um, yeah, you were kind of bossy," she said.

"And you went with your idea over any of ours," added Vikram. "Twice."

Nadia swallowed. "But . . . I thought we agreed that by using those ideas we'd have a better chance at winning the contest, right? You liked my ideas. At least, I thought you did."

Chloe sighed. "Your ideas were good, Nadia. They always are. But that's not the point. You hardly listened to us, hardly even gave us a chance to share our own ideas before barreling ahead with your own."

Vikram jumped in again. "We love working on projects with you, Nadia, but sometimes you get carried away. You try to figure out everything by yourself."

"But you don't have to," Sarah said. "That's what friends are for, right?"

Nadia didn't know what to say. She'd never thought about it like that before. Being a leader didn't mean telling people what to do or doing it all yourself. It was about guiding everyone else to come to a solution together.

She took a deep breath. "I'm sorry—really. I didn't mean to make you feel bad, like I wasn't interested in your ideas. I'm going to be better about that. And if I'm not, you have my permission to—"

"Burp in your face?" suggested Vikram. "I could get on board with that."

They all burst into laughter and Nadia let out a sigh of relief. Things were going to be okay with the Nerd Patrol.

"So . . ." Nadia grabbed the amulet again. "How is the project going? Did you figure out the costumes? Is there anything I can do to hel—ah!" She dropped the amulet just in time. *That was close.* This whole not-saying-help thing was going to be harder than she thought.

"Hey! You're wearing your hippo amulet again!" Chloe said.

"Yep," Nadia said. "I sort of took a break from all the Egyptian stuff for a few days, but now I'm back . . . and was wondering if I could come back to the project?"

The three friends exchanged another set of looks.

"Sorry, Nadia," Chloe said. "We decided not to do it. Without you and Adam, there was no way we'd get everything together by Saturday."

"Without Adam?" said Nadia. "You mean he . . ."

Sarah nodded. "He quit, too."

Nadia's heart sank.

"If it makes you feel better, Nadia," Vikram said, "Adam was never super into the project after that first day at your house. He told me he was thinking of dropping out even before the stuff that happened on Monday."

"What do you mean?" Nadia asked.

Vikram shrugged. "That's all he said."

Nadia thought back—there seemed to be a lot she didn't understand about her BFF these days. Why wasn't he into the project? Why did he want to be friends with Jason so badly? But she did know that she missed her best friend, terribly. And even though she still felt like he owed her an apology for calling her a know-it-all, she knew she owed him one, too, for keeping the comic book so long.

She turned to her friends. "If I talk to Adam and get him back on the project—are you guys still in? We'd have to work really fast, but I think we could figure something out, don't you?"

The three friends exchanged looks one more time and smiled.

"A-ffir-ma-tive," Vikram said in his robot voice.

Nadia stood on the doorstep of Adam's house and took a deep breath, then rang the bell. The comic book was under her arm. To give it to Adam meant no more dives into it with Titi, but she was okay with that. The magic stuff was definitely not for her.

Charlie answered the door wearing a sports jersey. Some basketball team, or maybe football. Nadia wasn't sure.

"Oh, hey, Nadia," he said, then turned to look over his shoulder. "Adam, there's someone here to see you!"

Adam bounded down the stairs, an expectant smile on his face. But when he spotted Nadia, his face fell.

"Hey, friend," she said. She held up the comic. "I think this belongs to you."

Adam was still for a moment, but then nodded. "Let's go out back," he said as he took the comic from her.

They walked to the backyard, and without even discussing it, they sat down on the porch swing where they had played countless games of cards and drunk lemonade over the years. Nadia pushed off and they swung back and forth.

"Thanks for the comic," Adam said, putting it on his lap.

Nadia nodded. "I'm sorry I didn't give it to you sooner. And . . . well, I wanted to say thank you again for standing up to Jason on Monday. That meant a lot to me."

"Yeah," Adam says. "What he said to you was awful. I can't be friends with someone who says stuff like that."

Nadia gulped, glad to hear her friend admit that.

A couple of moments passed without either of them speaking.

Finally, Nadia couldn't take it anymore.

"How come you wanted to be friends with him so badly anyway?" she asked. "He's funny, but not that funny."

Adam stopped the swing with his feet, then pushed off again. "You know Charlie, my stepdad?"

Nadia nodded.

"It's been sort of hard to get to know him. He's so into sports; half the time I feel like he's speaking a different language. I thought maybe Jason could help me learn some sports stuff so I could connect with Charlie more, you know?"

Huh. That actually made sense. It was sort of like how she asked her cousins to explain Egyptian pop culture memes to her so she could laugh along with them.

Nadia sighed. "I'm sorry Jason wasn't who you thought he was," she said.

Adam nodded. "It's a bummer."

They swung in silence for a few more minutes.

"So," Nadia said. "I talked to the Nerds about the project and apologized for how I acted. But they told me you quit. How come? I thought you were psyched about it."

Adam squinted at Nadia. "You're sure you won't get mad if I tell you?"

Nadia frowned. "I'll try."

Adam took a deep breath. "It was a hard project for me because I actually don't know much about my background. The rest of you guys all know who you are and where you're from. Especially you, since you were born in Egypt. I know it's hard for you sometimes—maybe a lot of the time—but I wish I had as clear a picture as you do of who I am. And I know you said to ask my parents, but I'm not in touch with my dad's side and my mom was adopted—"

"Really? I didn't know that," Nadia said.

"Yeah," Adam said. "So she doesn't have much info. Maybe her family is from Italy, maybe Germany . . . So the project . . . I just had a hard time getting into it."

Nadia paused. Sometimes she forgot that not everyone had such a strong connection to their heritage as she did.

"I wish you had told me," Nadia said.

"Yeah, me too," Adam said. "But you were all gung ho about the topic. That made it hard."

"I guess I'm not winning the Friend of the Year award," Nadia replied.

"Nope," said Adam. "But . . . I haven't been the best friend in the world either. I should have stood up to Jason a lot sooner."

"Yeah," Nadia said. "Maybe they should have just canceled the Friend of the Year awards this year." Then she grinned at Adam and they both burst into laughter. Adam grabbed the comic book to keep it from falling off his lap.

Suddenly, Nadia had an idea. A reckless, possibly very stupid idea. But if it could help her best friend, it would be worth it.

"Hey, can I borrow that comic book?" she asked.

"You mean the one you just gave me?" said Adam, holding it to his chest.

Nadia rolled her eyes. "Just give it to me." She grabbed the comic and held it up. "You know how I'm all about facts?"

"Obviously," Adam said.

"Well, here's one: Did you know that I also have some experience with magic?"

"Huh?"

Nadia grabbed the amulet and closed her eyes. "Help, Titi, help!" she said.

POOF! Titi appeared on the back cover of the comic book, hanging from some big letters.

"Good Giza, Nadia!" Titi exclaimed. "Talk about leaving me hanging! I was beginning to think I'd never see you again." He dropped down from the letters to the bottom of the comic and started pacing. "I was even considering skipping town—went on the internet to book a ticket and everything. The internet—boy, that's a scary place. I'd stay away if I were you." He froze, remembering where he was. "But here I am. Here you are! Wahooo!" He did three handsprings. "So, should we try out my new power? Where do you want to go first? The heyday of the Inca civilization? You've never seen so much gold, I promise. Or the fall of Rome? No, I take that back. Even more depressing than the internet. Where should we go, huh? Oh, I can't wait!"

Adam was staring at Titi, his mouth hanging open, just as Nadia's had been when she first met Titi. The teacher hadn't noticed Adam yet. He was too busy bouncing from corner to corner of the comic.

"Actually," Nadia said, "we're hoping you can tell us where to go."

Titi paused. "We? Who's we?"

Nadia pointed to Adam.

Titi looked up and his eyes went wide. "Well, steal my scribal palette and call me a dope! Is this Adam? You're introducing me to your friends, Nadia?" He spun three cartwheels in a row, then offered Adam a fist bump. "How the heck are you, Adam?"

Adam returned the fist bump, a look of utter shock on his face.

"So, Titi," Nadia said. "Adam doesn't know where he comes from. You think you could use the comic to help show him his family's hist—"

"The sixth solution?! Woo-hoo! Yes, yes, yes! I just have to do a little research. Hang on!"

POOF! He disappeared.

"Wh-wh-what was that?" Adam stammered. "Was that for real? What's going on?"

"Just wait," Nadia said. She opened the comic and they both stared at it.

POOF! Titi reappeared.

"Hang on to your hats, kids—"

"But I'm not wearing a h—" Adam said. Knowing what was coming next, Nadia grabbed Adam's arm before he could finish.

WHOOSH!

Ten minutes later, they whooshed back into Adam's yard.

"That. Was. AMAZING!" Adam yelled. "I'M AUSTRIAN!" He jumped up and spun around like Julie Andrews in that musical about the singing Austrian family, *The Sound of Music*. "*The hills are alive, with the sound of muuuuuusic . . .*" he sang.

Nadia joined in. Titi grinned at them from the comic book as Nadia and Adam spun around and around until they fell down in the grass with laughter.

"I can see why you kept the comic book now," Adam said. "And I'm glad you finally decided to show it to me."

Nadia beamed. Maybe a little magic every once in a while was okay after all.

Adam grew serious. "I had no idea that my great-great-grandparents had to flee their country so my great-great-grandpa could avoid being drafted into the German army during World War II. They just up and left and came to a country where they didn't know anybody. That's pretty crazy."

Nadia nodded, then filled him on what she'd learned about her own family history the night before.

Adam turned to her. "Huh. We have more in common than we thought," he said.

Nadia sat up in the grass. That was like what her mother said. *Find something in common. Show them you aren't so different after all.*

"What if we could find something in common with Jason?" she suddenly said.

Adam stared at her. "You're not suggesting we take Jason into the comic, are you?"

Nadia shook her head. "No way." Her shoulders sagged. "Never mind. We have to get to work on the project anyway. There's so much to do before Saturday!"

Adam smiled. "Hold on. Maybe there is a way to get through to Jason. I have an idea."

Chapter Thirteen

Everything was set. The rest of the Nerd Patrol had been totally into the idea. They had stayed up most of Friday night working on it, but at last they were done. Adam had the comic. Everyone had their cue cards. The star of their presentation didn't yet know he'd be the star, but assuming he cooperated, everything would fall into place.

Nadia fidgeted in her seat. She sat in the first row of the museum auditorium, along with the other presenters. Somewhere behind her, her parents sat with the other Nerd Patrol parents and more than a hundred audience members. Principal Taylor was there, and Ms. Arena, and many of her classmates. Ms. Gilson— to Nadia's surprise—was the MC; she had a surprising amount of stage presence. The board members sat to the side of the stage, whispering among themselves and taking notes.

Nadia looked down at her cue cards and Titi smiled up at her. He gave her a wink and a thumbs-up. Titi was about to play a big role—not that the other Nerds knew anything about that. Nadia and Adam had decided to keep Titi a secret between them for now.

That was the part of the idea that Adam had to sell Nadia on the most. Because if Titi helped them, and they actually got through to Jason, that would be the seventh solution. That meant Titi would get his freedom, and who knew what would happen after that? Nadia hated the thought of potentially losing her wise-but-wacky friend.

In the end, though, Nadia decided Titi playing a role in their project was worth it if it helped them get through to Jason. And besides, Titi totally deserved his freedom after everything he'd done for Nadia.

Everyone clapped politely after the Far-Reaching Effects of the Continental Congress presentation. Nadia had made note of one or two fun facts, but overall, it had been pretty boring. Titi gave her a grimace and a thumbs-down from her cue cards.

"And now," Ms. Gilson said, "we have Inspirational Moments in American Sports History, led by Jason Flanagan!"

Behind them, someone whooped loudly. Adam gave Nadia a knowing smile—that had to be Charlie.

Jason walked onstage, dressed in a football uniform and helmet. A football flew out of the wings in a beautiful arcing spiral and Jason caught it neatly.

Behind Jason, an image of the American flag fluttered onto a big screen. Patriotic music started to play.

"Professional sports have long been an important part of American life," Jason began. "People love to root for their favorite teams. Americans gather in stadiums, in sports bars, and in living rooms, watching their favorite teams together. There are intense rivalries, even among family members.

"But throughout our country's history, there have been times when sports have built connections between people, rather than tearing them apart."

He held up the football. "The first Super Bowl held after the September eleventh attacks was held in January 2002. During the halftime show, millions of Americans watched as the names of the 2,977 victims were displayed."

Nadia blinked, surprised by Jason's strong start.

Aiden stepped onstage next, dressed in a baseball

uniform. He held up his glove and someone tossed him a ball. "During World War II, the All-American Girls Professional Baseball League was formed. Even though they had to wear lipstick and attend charm school, the women were fierce and talented players and kept Americans entertained during the war. For the first time, American women, men, and children came together to root for professional women athletes. The players paved the way for the advancement of women's sports."

"Cool," said Nadia under her breath.

After that, Mike spoke of African American track and field athlete Jesse Owens winning four gold medals at the 1936 Olympics. He broke several records, but it was a victory in a bigger way, too: Hitler had claimed Germans would win all the gold medals because "Aryans"—what he called German white people—were superior, and here was a person of color proving him wrong. It brought together not only Americans but people worldwide who were fighting against Hitler's cruel politics.

Jason stepped forward again. "These are only a few examples of how sports brought our country together. In wartime, against tyrants, in times of grief, and in times of joy. These were not simply games. These were moments in American history, never to be forgotten."

The audience burst into applause. On the cue cards in Nadia's lap, Titi sniffed loudly.

"So moving," he whispered, dramatically wiping away a tear.

But Nadia sighed, her brow furrowed. *Not simply games . . .*

Her words from the ice cream parlor came rushing back: *It's just a stupid game.* Jason had delivered the deepest insult to her that day, one that attacked the very core of who she was. But Nadia realized she had also insulted him. It wasn't the same, but her words must have hurt.

Around her, the crowd was clapping wildly for Jason and his team. Nadia joined in.

"And next up," said Ms. Gilson, "is Immigreat, led by Nadia Youssef!"

"Here we go," Nadia whispered to Titi as they made their way to the stage. "Behave, okay?"

The Nerds climbed onstage. They wore street clothes and each held a different prop in their hands. Adam headed over to the projector they'd set up in front of the stage earlier. He opened up his laptop, then slyly placed the comic book on top. He plugged in his phone, too, and set it up to video the comic book, which would feed to the projector. He didn't turn the projector on just yet, though. When everything was set, he gave Nadia the cue.

"America is a nation of immigrants," Nadia began. "Our little group here represents five different generations of immigrants from six different countries. My name is Nadia and I am an immigrant from Egypt," she said.

"My name is Vikram and my parents emigrated from India," said Vikram.

"My name is Chloe and my grandparents emigrated from Jamaica and Barbados."

"My name is Sarah and my great-grandparents emigrated from Korea," said Sarah.

"My name is Adam and my great-great-grandparents emigrated from Austria. Our original plan today was to wow you with the amazing stories of the accomplishments of immigrants from these countries. Authors, activists, scientists, astronauts."

There was some laughter from one end of the front row, where Jason's group was sitting. Nadia couldn't read lips, but was pretty sure Aiden said "Boring!" to Jason. Oddly, Jason was ignoring him.

"But our country's story is not just that of scientists and authors and inventors," Vikram continued. "It is also the story of countless ordinary people who came here to make this nation their new home."

"Can we have a volunteer from the audience?" Sarah asked.

"Maybe someone who just gave a good

presentation?" suggested Chloe. She gestured to Jason. "Jason, would you mind helping us out?"

Jason looked very surprised, but also . . . intrigued?

Adam pointed to him. "Let's give a big round of applause to our volunteer, Jason Flanagan." The audience clapped and Jason began to warm up, taking a little bow. He climbed up onstage.

Vikram handed Jason a wig of long brown hair. The audience laughed. Jason held it up and made a face but then shrugged and put it on.

Sarah stepped forward, holding a shawl. Jason allowed her to drape it over his shoulders. The crowd clapped to show their approval.

"Just stand here for now," Vikram said to Jason. "Your part comes in a minute."

Jason nodded, happy to be in the spotlight once again.

Nadia held her cue cards up in front of her face for just a moment.

"Ready to do your thing, Titi?" she asked.

"You bet," Titi said. Then he disappeared.

Nadia nodded at Adam and he flipped on the projector. A comic book panel appeared on the back wall of the stage, showing a sweeping countryside. It looked just as it had when Titi had shown it to Adam and Nadia two nights ago, only now it was much, much bigger, thanks to the projector. Nadia and Adam knew the artwork was done with Titi's magic, but the other Nerds didn't. Adam and Nadia had made up some explanation about finding an app online that would generate comic book art and even animation when you typed in specific info. Adam was so good at tech stuff, the other Nerds believed their story.

"It all started during the potato famine of 1845," Sarah began. "Otherwise known as the Great Hunger. One million men, women, and children died during the seven-year famine that swept through Ireland."

A second comic panel appeared next to the first as Chloe went on. "With the difficult choice between starving to death or fleeing to an uncertain fate, two million Irish people set off for the United States of America. Many ended up in Boston and New York City." The panel showed people on a ship, arriving in the NYC harbor.

"One of these immigrants was a young woman named Rose McGurk," said Vikram, gesturing to Jason in his wig. "She discovered that life was harsh in her new city of Boston. Many people tried to take advantage of the immigrants. They stole the little money that they had. Rotten landlords would charge high rents, then cram ten people into a room meant for one."

As Vikram spoke, Titi made a third panel appear in the comic book and it was projected onto the back wall,

this time right behind Jason. It showed the inside of a crammed apartment.

The audience gasped. It was working perfectly—Jason looked like he was in the scene!

Titi was in the scene, too. Only he didn't look like Titi. He looked like a grumpy old lady. Titi's newest power was his ability to change his appearance. To everyone's delight, he suddenly moved and pretended to bump into Jason. He wagged a finger at him. The audience roared.

Nadia continued. "With many new immigrants in town, people had to compete for jobs. There was a great rivalry between the new immigrants and the working-class Bostonians. People began hanging signs that said, 'No Irish Need Apply.'"

Behind Jason, Titi made the artwork change to a storefront featuring a similar sign. Titi appeared again, this time playing the part of an angry shop owner. He pointed at Jason and silently yelled at him.

The Nerds were his voice. "People told Rose, 'Go back where you came from!'" Chloe said.

"'You don't belong here,'" said Sarah.

"'This is OUR country. Not YOURS,'" said Vikram.

Nadia had been nervous about this moment. Would Jason say something rude and ruin everything? But Jason was silent, his brow furrowed.

"Rose prevailed, though," said Nadia. "She found a

job. She got married, and she and her husband saved up their money."

Images of all this flashed behind them. Chloe handed Jason a bouquet of flowers. Titi, appearing as a young Irishman in a suit and tie, stood proudly next to Jason. He gazed at Jason adoringly.

Vikram continued. "When the couple had enough money, they started their own boardinghouse for recent immigrants—a place of safety and comfort. It was a lot of work, but they were up for the challenge."

Nadia grabbed the shawl off Jason's shoulders and tied an apron around his waist.

"Rose ended up being a successful hotel owner and always gave back to the community," Chloe said. She shook "Rose's" hand heartily in thanks.

"Rose and her husband had a few children," said Sarah as some ridiculously adorable children appeared on the screen. Titi, of course, was the cutest one, toddling around Jason. "Their children grew up and had children of their own. And they had children, and so on . . . until Rose McGurk's great-great-great-grandson Thomas met a woman named Melissa."

Nadia stole a glance at Jason's face. It looked like a realization was dawning.

Vikram picked up where Sarah left off.

"And Thomas and Melissa had a son named . . ."

Chapter Fourteen

Jason Flanagan."

The audience gasped, then let out a big cheer. Jason had a shocked look on his face.

Titi, his part of the presentation done, hopped back to Nadia's notecards. He quickly pushed a few letters around to spell out, *We did it!* Nadia smiled, but they weren't done yet.

"So you see," said Nadia as the audience quieted and Titi put the letters back, "unless you are Native American, we *all* have an immigrant story in our past. Each of us is here today because one of our ancestors came to America and started a life for their family."

Over at the projector, Adam switched to projecting his laptop screen, which flashed with images of flags from different countries, followed by the American flag.

Sarah continued. "What if someone told your ancestor to 'go back where you came from' and that ancestor did? Some of us might not be here. Whether they came five hundred years ago or five months ago, by boat or airplane, by choice or—in the case of enslaved people—by force, we are here because of them. All of us were strangers in this land at some point."

"To some families—whether fifth- or first-generation American—their background is important to them, and that's okay," said Adam, coming to join the group. "And then there's some of us, like me, whose families no longer relate to the countries we came from. And that's okay, too. New things come to define us. Things like the hobbies you pursue or what type of business your family owns—"

"Or," Nadia said, going off script for a moment, "the sports teams you like." She smiled at Jason. Adam nodded at Charlie in the crowd.

"My Egyptian background is as important to me as . . . football is to some people's families," Nadia said. "We all have many things that define us—ethnicity, religion, our likes and dislikes. These things make us who we are. They are a part of us. And they matter. But we cannot forget that we were all immigrants once. That almost everything 'American' was originally the idea of someone whose family came from South America, or

Europe, or Asia, or Australia, or Central America, or the Caribbean, or the Middle East, or Africa, or elsewhere."

"Our ancestors went through a lot to get us here," Sarah said. "There are some things—hard things—we wish they hadn't had to go through." She looked to the others so they could finish together as they had practiced. "We can't go back and change that history . . ."

"But we can make sure we don't repeat it," they all said together.

The crowd burst into cheers. Then, to Nadia's delight, the audience rose to their feet. A standing ovation!

The Nerd Patrol all looked at one another, huge grins on their faces. The friends put their arms around one another and took a deep bow.

Then Nadia reached over and grabbed Jason's hand so he could take the second bow with them.

Chapter Fifteen

Monday morning, Nadia went downstairs to grab some breakfast.

"There she is," Baba said from the breakfast table. "My inspirational daughter."

Nadia rolled her eyes. "Cut it out, Baba."

"Nope," Mama said. "We will not. We are impressed by you, habibti. You went up on that stage proud of who you are."

Nadia looked at her mom, then her dad. She suddenly felt overwhelmed with gratitude for the sacrifices they had made for her. Still, she didn't want to get too sappy right before school.

"Thanks, you guys," she said just as she slipped out the door. "Thanks for everything."

Nadia was happy to see Adam waiting for her on the corner as if nothing had ever happened.

"So guess what?" Adam said as they started walking. "I watched the big game on Sunday with Charlie!"

"Oh, that's great," Nadia said. "Who won?"

"Do you care?" asked Adam.

"Well, I . . . Nope," Nadia admitted.

Adam laughed. "Good. Because I can't even remember which teams were playing. But Charlie taught me loads of stuff. And then we watched a couple of episodes of Doctor Who. He seemed to like it!"

"Awesome," Nadia said. "Hey, did you know that thirteen different actors have portrayed Doctor Who since the show first went on the air in 1963?"

"Actually, I did know that," Adam said. "Because I'm the one who told you!"

"Oh, right," Nadia said, laughing.

"So want to come over later and do a comic book dive?" Adam asked. "Where should Titi take us next?"

Titi. Nadia wasn't sure what was going to happen with him. Had they gotten through to Jason? Only time would tell. But another question loomed: If they got through to Jason and Titi was freed, would Titi stick around? Nadia hated to think about having to say goodbye to the tiny teacher she'd come to think of as a friend.

At school, Nadia and Adam parted ways to put their books in their lockers. Nadia was just slamming hers shut when she felt a tap on her shoulder.

"Oh, hey, Jason," Nadia said. Jason nervously shifted his backpack from one shoulder to the other.

"I . . . I just wanted to say sorry for what I said to you at the ice cream place. It wasn't cool at all."

Nadia tried to hide her surprise. They were hoping to affect Jason with their presentation, but she wasn't expecting an apology. Her parents had warned her that people like Jason didn't change overnight.

"I'm sorry for ruining your project, too," Jason continued. "You guys did awesome anyway, though. We really thought you were going to win." He raised an eyebrow.

Nadia laughed. "We did, too. Congratulations, by the way."

"Thanks," Jason said.

It was a hard pill to swallow—Jason's team beating hers. But the judges had said it was a really tough decision. Nadia figured the subject matter had something to do with it. An exhibit on sports was sure to draw visitors to the museum. She had to admit that she herself was even looking forward to going and learning more about all the stuff Jason's team mentioned.

"I'm sorry I said football was stupid," Nadia said. "I know it's important to you."

Jason nodded just as the bell rang for homeroom. They headed to Ms. Arena's classroom. Inside, Nadia walked to her usual desk near Adam and Sarah and was surprised to find Jason following her. He stood there awkwardly while Nadia put her bag on the back of her chair.

"Um, can I help you with something?" Nadia joked.

Jason looked down at his feet. "Do you think maybe I could sit with you guys at lunch again? I always learn something new when I sit with you nerds."

Adam and Sarah turned to Nadia, letting her make the decision.

Jason seemed genuine, but if he was going to sit with them, she wanted to set some boundaries. Nadia held up her lunch bag. "Do you promise not to make fun of my food? I brought *mahshi* today, so it might be a challenge."

Jason paused. "I promise. Well, I promise to try. Sometimes it's hard to know what's okay and what's not okay to say, you know?"

"We can help you with that," Nadia said.

"Totally," Sarah added. "Ooh! What if there's a way we could signal to each other when something's not cool. A code word or a hand sign or something. If you— or anyone—says something disrespectful, we just do the thing."

"I like it," Jason said. "Does that work for you, Nadia?"

Nadia nodded. "So long as the thing isn't burping in my face," she said with a laugh, remembering Vikram's suggestion. "How about *hamar*?" Nadia said. She pronounced the word like *Homer* in *Homer Simpson*. "It means donkey in Arabic."

She thought Jason might be insulted, but he just laughed. "It's perfect," he said. "You can say 'Jason, don't be such a *hamar*,' and you won't get in trouble."

"Hey, did you know that pound for pound, a donkey is stronger than a horse?" Nadia asked.

"See?" Jason said. "That's what I'm talking about! Always learning something new with you guys!"

"Careful what you ask for, Jason," Adam joked. "Nadia's got hundreds—no, thousands—more fun facts she can share."

"Sure do," Nadia said with a smile. "And that's a fact."

Nadia found her seat in Mr. Decker's social studies class and flipped open her notebook . . . and there stood Titi Presley.

"Titi! What are you doing?" she whispered. "No showing up in front of my classmates, remember?"

"We have to talk," Titi whispered back.

"After class," Nadia said.

"Nope, now," Titi replied.

And to her unbelieving eyes, Titi reached up— and off the page. His sparkly arm was poking out of the notebook!

Nadia slammed the notebook shut and hurried to 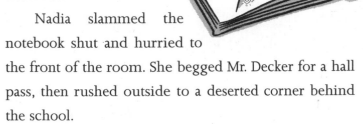 the front of the room. She begged Mr. Decker for a hall pass, then rushed outside to a deserted corner behind the school.

"Something's going on," Titi said. "Something big. I think I'm going to be free! Quick! Put your notebook on the ground. And stand back!"

Nadia dropped the notebook in the grass and took a few steps back. Her heart was beating hard.

At first it was just his tiny hand again, reaching up. But then . . . POOF! A cloud of smoke rose up out of the notebook. When the smoke cleared, a human Titi was standing right in front of her!

Nadia coughed and blinked. "You're, uh, taller than I thought," she said.

Titi laughed, patting his sparkly white jumpsuit from head to toe. "I can't believe I'm me again!

Wahooooo!" He went to do a back handspring . . . and landed on his head.

"Ooof," Nadia said, running to help him up. "I guess human Titi can't do gymnastics?"

"I guess not," he replied. "Oh well. Small price to pay for being free. Holy hawks and dung beetles! I still can't believe it!"

Nadia laughed. Would Titi ever run out of those silly phrases? And would she get to hear any more of them?

"So, um . . . what's next?" Nadia asked.

Titi spun in a slow circle, taking everything in. His jumpsuit sparkled in the sunlight. "I guess this is goodbye," he said.

Nadia hung her head.

Titi's face softened. "Oh, Nadia. Of course I don't want to leave you. But my work here is done. It's time for me to go off and experience the world. Actually go see all the places I spent centuries just hearing about. I must contemplate the changes to the world since my last time walking on this earth!"

"I'll miss you, Titi," Nadia said, a catch in her voice. "You've taught me so much."

"I know," said Titi.

Nadia laughed. Classic Titi.

"So where will you go first?" she asked.

"Glad you asked," Titi said, excitement flashing

across his face, "I plan to visit a majestic place. A sacred site of pilgrimage, to honor a mighty king. It's called . . . Graceland!"

Nadia rolled her eyes. Of course Titi would want to visit Elvis Presley's historic home.

"Well," said Nadia. "You're certainly dressed for it."

Epilogue

POOF!

The royal magician looked around. After two thousand years of being confined to that amulet—the hippo's head, to be precise, not its behind, he was happy to report—he was finally seeing the outside world.

He could still hardly believe that the elder had turned out to be a magician even more powerful than he was. The elder's words had haunted him these last two thousand years:

> "Royal magician, I am sorry to do this, but you leave me no choice. The teacher's jest did not warrant your cruelty. I amend your magic so there is a way to break the spell. If a young Egyptian makes contact and says the word help, the teacher shall face trials but eventually be released—"
>
> "Don't you dare—" the royal magician started to say, but the elder cut him off.

"—which you should care about, because I condemn you to the same fate! Your freedom shall be
linked to the teacher's—"

And before the royal magician knew it, he was
screaming as everything went black.

The teacher—the magician couldn't even say his name,
that's how much he hated him—had certainly taken his time
facing the trials, hadn't he? Helping those dumb kids—what a
waste of energy.

The magician had been paying attention to the teacher's
interactions, though. He had started forming a plan.

He looked up at the blue sky for the first time in over two
thousand years. But this sight did not bring him joy or wonder.
He had one thing and one thing only on his mind: revenge.

About the Authors

Photo by Andrew Frasz

Bassem Youssef, aka the Jon Stewart of the Arab World, was a heart surgeon in his home country of Egypt before becoming the host of *AlBernameg*, the first political satire show in the Middle East. He has appeared on *The Daily Show*, *The Late Show with Stephen Colbert*, and other late-night shows, and was also featured in TIME 100, *Time* magazine's list of the one hundred most influential people in the world. He lives in Los Angeles with his family.

Photo by Cindy Johnson Photography

Catherine R. Daly has written many books for young readers, including the Petal Pushers middle-grade series and the Disney Fairies chapter book *Prilla and the Butterfly Lie*. She lives in New York City with her family and their very energetic Boston terrier, Jack.

About the Artist

Photo courtesy of the artist

Douglas Holgate is the illustrator of the New York Times bestselling series The Last Kids on Earth by Max Brallier, as well as the PlanetTad series, the Cheesie Mack series, and many other books for young readers. He has illustrated countless comics, as well as the graphic novels *Wires and Nerve, Volume One* by Marissa Meyer and *Clem Hetherington and the Ironwood Race*, cocreated with writer Jen Breach. Douglas lives in Melbourne, Australia, with his family and a large dog who is possibly part polar bear.

31901066311913